MANTILLA BLUFF

MANTILLA BLUFF

•

NANCY COOK-SENN

AVALON BOOKS
THOMAS BOUREGY AND COMPANY, INC.
401 LAFAYETTE STREET
NEW YORK, NEW YORK 10003

Fic
Coo
R

© Copyright 1994 by Nancy Cook-Senn
Library of Congress Catalog Card Number: 94–96440
ISBN 0–8034–9084–4

PRINTED IN THE UNITED STATES OF AMERICA
ON ACID-FREE PAPER
BY HADDON CRAFTSMEN, SCRANTON, PENNSYLVANIA

MANTILLA BLUFF

Chapter One

Andrea Zanovya pressed the gas pedal a little harder. Beautiful and dramatic as it was, the rolling, mesquite-dotted prairie was becoming monotonous. She wondered for the hundredth time why she was doing this. Why was she traveling all the way from New York to Amarillo, Texas—a place she'd hardly heard of—to meet people she didn't know, to settle an inheritance from a man she'd never met? And why was she driving alone into the silent Texas panhandle prairie?

Andrea had always thought of herself as an exceptionally mature and independent young woman, but when she'd arrived at the small airport and Mr. Blackburn had not been there to meet her, she realized that she felt uncomfortable traveling solo. She couldn't remember the last time she had flown anywhere without the rest of the ballet company, or Nigel at least, with her.

She had lived her whole life as part of a dance company. First, traveling with her parents' tours, then residing for a year or two at a time with ballet companies in New York and other eastern cities. Now here she was alone in Texas, of all places—sweeping plains, rough-riding he-men, rousing adventure in the wide-open spaces—with her newly and mysteriously acquired wealth. She chuckled at the unreality of it. What was a roughriding he-man, anyway?

No, fantasies were not for Andrea Zanovya the dedicated, the disciplined craftsman. She once again felt very foolish for having agreed to come to Texas at all. Why waste what precious little time she had before the new season's rehearsals began?

She was sure Amarillo was the edge of the civilized world. It was certainly beyond her world and she knew instinctively that she didn't belong here. But Mr. Blackburn had told her repeatedly in his telephone calls that inheriting a working farm and ranch complete with mineral rights could be tricky. It would be easier and faster if she could spend some time in Texas, he assured her. So just when she should be making the personal contacts that could help her get the lead role in "Giselle," she had waited alone in a Texas airport for a stranger who never appeared.

She had waited, paced, worried, and fumed. *Okay, Mr. Blackburn,* she had thought, *I'm here. Where are you? You were so eager for me to come to Texas that I expected to be met. I can maneuver my way through any city on the East Coast but I hope you don't expect me to strike out across the desert on my own.*

But that's what she had done. The car-rental agency gave her a seven-year-old sedan with stiff power steering and a map marking the best route to a tiny dot called Perico. "Since you're in a hurry, take the Boys' Ranch road," the young clerk had drawled, making the last word two gliding syllables. "You can drive a lot faster on this road since there's not much traffic. But don't blink or you'll sail right past Perico!"

Andrea saw what the young woman meant. From the airport the edge of Amarillo quickly faded to sandy rolling plains. She met fewer and fewer cars the further she drove from the city. The growing isolation and the sinking sun made her nervous. And that made her angrier at Mr. Blackburn.

She drove faster and silently grumbled at the ranch manager who had stood her up. *I didn't want to come out here. You insisted. Old Mr. Merrick wanted me to see the place, you said—an old man's dying request.*

Nigel wanted me to come. A nice little change of scenery to calm my nerves and get my mind off Boston and the contract, he said.

Well, I don't care about old Mr. Merrick, whoever he was, she thought, *or about inheriting some stupid chunk of desert when I have a major career change to consider. And this change of scenery is* not *relaxing me.*

Suddenly, the scenery changed. As the old car bounced over a rise, she saw the highway split sharply to the right and left in an intersection at the bottom of the slope. Andrea had squinted into the sun staring hypnotically at the faded blacktop, for so long that she almost missed the road sign. Turn left for Vega, and right for some other place. She was traveling too fast to read it and too fast to handle a sharp turn, she realized.

She slammed her foot on the spongy brakes, but for several seconds the heavy car didn't respond. She stomped the brakes again. The car groaned and slowed at the stop sign, but didn't stop. Andrea tried to steer to the right; the rear tires skidded left. The car lunged jaggedly across the intersection, lifting Andrea off the seat with each bounce, and nosed at a crazy angle into the embankment of the sandy ditch on the other side of the road.

Thank goodness there was no traffic. Andrea took a deep, calming breath and watched the dust settle. That turn wasn't marked on the map. *I hate cars,* she griped inwardly. *I like subways and trains. And taxis.*

She shifted into reverse, looked both directions, spotted a sign down the road, and eased off the brake. Nothing happened. She gently pressed the accelerator. The motor rumbled contentedly.

Andrea pressed harder, the motor growled, and the tires whined and sent up a cloud of sandy dust before shivering deeper into the sand. *Oh, great,* she thought, pounding the steering wheel once. *How do I call the auto club from here—by smoke signal?*

Andrea tried twisting the wheels left and then right. Finally, she stepped out and looked at the front of the car. What wasn't nuzzling the side of the ditch didn't look damaged. She looked at the tires. How could a few inches of sandy soil trap a big, powerful car like that?

"Okay, you ugly behemoth, what now?" she asked the car aloud, kicking at it in irritation. "I can't walk to the nearest garage. Out here that would probably take me six days. You're too heavy to push even if I could get between you and the hill. You need to be out of the sand."

She suddenly felt very thirsty. Just her imagination, she decided, but the sun *was* getting awfully low on the horizon. Andrea wasn't used to being this alone in this much space. She felt a shiver at the spooky emptiness. To fight the growing fear of isolation, she tried to be practical, not emotional. The tires needed to be out of the sand, she reasoned, or on firmer sand—on top of the sand.

She needed to wedge something under the tires for traction. The only thing Andrea could think of to use out in the wilderness were the clothes in her suitcase, which she wasn't about to ruin. Or branches from some scrubby bushes nearby, she thought.

She was cheered by her flash of ingenuity, until she tried to slide between the wires of the fence separating her from the plentiful mesquite. The barbs caught her clothes, her back, her legs, her hose, and her hair. She untangled her way to the other side, cursing the fence, the car, the road map, fate, and Mr. Blackburn, whose fault it really was for not meeting her at the airport. She jerked out the bands that no longer held back her long chestnut hair, shook it loosely around her shoulders, and assessed the damage.

Control, Andrea, she reminded herself. *Always discipline and control. The skirt can be repaired. You're not really bleeding; they're only scratches. The hose are gone anyway, so save the heels.* She kicked off her shoes and approached the nearest clump of mesquite. She gathered the few broken branches that lay loose and then bent a live branch to break it off. It was much tougher than she expected. But it looked so dry and brittle. She moved her hand up where the branch was thinner and tried again. She tried another branch, put down her load, and tugged with both hands.

She tried another bush. She wrestled with several wiry branches, getting more exasperated as each one resisted her efforts.

I hate Texas, she thought. *I hate cars, I hate inheritances from strangers, I hate waiting for audition results.* She rubbed her tender, scratched hands and strangled a branch with one last great effort. *And I hate Mr. Blackburn!*

Her heels slid into the sand, plowing small furrows, and she thumped to the ground, straddling the stubborn branch. Then she heard the sound.

Andrea looked over her shoulder toward the car. A battered pickup truck idled next to her nose-dive rental. A figure in a cowboy hat hunched down, peering at her through the side window. She didn't feel confident and self-reliant now. She was embarrassed to be caught in such a ridiculous position—and barefoot at that.

The figure moved and Andrea scrambled to her feet, pulling her skirt down and dusting off. His sudden appearance out of an empty prairie gave her an uneasy feeling. She didn't know whether to welcome or fear the presence of a stranger. Fear, she decided instantly as the figure slid out of the truck and slouched toward the fence. Andrea longed for the safe, sturdy enclosure of the rental car, now too far on the other side of him for a quick dash. She felt vulnerable without her purse, her handy canister of Mace, or at least her shoes with their potentially lethal spike heels.

She hurriedly tried to size up the threat of the stranger who ambled toward her, separating her from the road and both vehicles. He was tall, lanky, and wearing very dusty jeans and an old plaid shirt with the sleeves ripped off, revealing muscular shoulders and arms sun-bronzed and hardened by labor.

If she had encountered him on a city street she could have judged his intent by how he moved in relation to the crowd, the buildings, and the street. She could have looked at his eyes to see if he was high on drugs or if he seemed crazy. But she had no idea how to combat a Texas mugger. Under the bent brim of his battered straw hat she could only see a square, tanned jawline and a straight, wide mouth with a hint of a smirk.

"Nice day for pickin' screwbeans," he drawled.

At the sound of his voice, deep and slow and laced with sarcasm, Andrea panicked. Her pulse raced with adrenaline as she realized there was no place to run. *I'm going to be killed and left in the desert, the sun bleaching my bones,* she thought. One always heard about things like that happening in the middle of nowhere.

"Do you always park that way?" he asked.

"I missed the turn," she answered numbly.

"So I see." He walked back and retrieved a heavy chain from the back of his truck.

Andrea's knees wobbled. She hastily gathered her few sticks of mesquite. *Like I can defend myself with these things,* she chided herself. She felt very weak, vulnerable, and disheveled in her stocking feet. She wiped one tear from her eye, took a deep breath for courage, and looked back toward him.

He was sliding easily under the back of her car. One end of the chain already was fastened to his truck. He stood, opened her car door, and adjusted the wheel and gear shift. It took only a few more seconds for his truck to pull the car out of its sandy notch and back onto the road. He stepped out of the truck again and examined the front of the car.

"Nothin' major, but I better tow it to Hartley. You should've waited for me, Miss Zanovya."

Miss Zanovya?

"You're Blackburn?" She hadn't meant to sound so condescending, nor look so disparagingly at his appearance.

"Last time I checked," he said dryly.

Andrea felt bewildered, embarrassed, relieved, and outraged all at once. She opened her mouth to speak, wondering what would come out of it first. "I did wait for you at the airport, Mr. Blackburn. But when you didn't come I thought I might as well have a rental car at my disposal in Perico and save you a return trip to Amarillo."

She looked at his attire and couldn't avoid adding sarcastically, "I'm sure the long drive is very difficult for you to manage."

"Not as difficult as for some."

Andrea felt her face burn with embarrassment.

He met her at the barbed wire fence, pushed one strand down with a dusty boot, and pulled another up to permit her to slide through.

"Allow me, Miss." He tipped his hat and Andrea caught an amused gleam in his eye before he settled the Stetson back on his brow.

Andrea dropped her mesquite, yanked her scarf free from the barb where it had fluttered all this time, and stepped as regally as she could under the circumstances through the gap. Andrea felt her face flush again. She tugged to keep her slim skirt down. As she straightened she gave him a quick glance. His mouth and jaw twitched in an effort to remain expressionless as he handed her the shoes she'd forgotten.

He sauntered to the truck and held the passenger door open for her, giving her his hand to assist her into the cab of the pickup. Was there a mocking quality to his courteous manner or did she just feel very foolish to be in this awkward situation? A few hours ago she was sanely, routinely doing her barre exercises in the studio. And she was clean. Now she was sitting, tattered and dirty, in a dusty old truck trying to find room for her feet between some greasy tools and a box marked *Veterinary Supply*.

She draped her long legs over the box and squirmed a little to the left when a long rip in the dry, cracked vinyl upholstery pinched her leg. Blackburn frowned at her position and jerked the gearshift in the floor. Andrea tugged at her short skirt again just as he shifted into second gear and bumped her leg with a rough hand.

She felt uncomfortably close to the somber stranger as they drove. She didn't want to look at him because her

ver. "How far is it to Mantilla Bluff?" she asked im-
atiently.

"For you, about a million miles and yesterdays."

Andrea opened her mouth for a sharp retort, but
uldn't think of one. She didn't know what he meant
that remark and she was too tired for any more verbal
arring.

She wondered again why she had left New York before
aring the results of her audition. She had no sensible
son for journeying all this way. Surely any legal busi-
s could be handled through lawyers and she certainly
w she didn't belong in Texas, so far from everything
had ever known.

he barely noticed the miles of rugged scenery they
ed. Her mind returned to New York. She had spent
xhausting summer dancing with a special ballet fes-
. The work had been artistically challenging and she
he had reached a high point in her career. Her per-
ances had impressed the artistic director of the Bos-
Ballet and now she might have a chance to sign a
act with that company for the new season.

e saw herself dancing "Giselle." It would demand
st of her technically and she was ready. But the
lso called for a good actress and she was a bit
d about that. In matters of technique, precision,
ntrol, the training she had received from her parents
d that she was one of the best young ballerinas in
untry. Her father, the masterful Andres Zanov,
believed that was all she needed to be a great artist.

of course, Andrea knew she could never be as
dancer as her mother had been. Lorraina Powell
a had danced with perfect technique, but she also
ed a passion that made each role and each per-
e a breathtaking heartache for her adoring daugh-

eyes always lingered on the faded jeans hugging his thigh
or the muscular chest peeking out of his ripped shirt.
Andrea didn't want to talk, but this awkward silence was
worse. Finally she managed to say, "I waited and then
decided there must have been a . . . a miscommunication
about my arrival."

They both stared straight ahead.

Five miles later he said, "One of the ladies wanted to
meet you, but her mother had a spell and, at the last
minute, she had to call me to come instead. We're calvin'
and it took me a while to get on the road. But you've
got another healthy white-face heifer."

"Oh, I see. That's . . . good." Andrea didn't know
what else to say. She was sorry she had been rude—it
wasn't dignified—but she was still too irritated and embarrassed to apologize.

Fortunately, they had arrived in a tiny town. Blackburn
left her car for repair at the town's one garage with a few
words and a handshake with the mechanic.

"They'll dust it off and get it back to Amarillo for
you," he told her as he tossed her bags into the back of
the truck.

"But I'll need it to get myself back to Amarillo," she
protested as she watched her expensive suitcase rock on
the rough bed of the pickup, then fall sideways and crum-
ple her garment bag. "I must return east immediately.
I'd like to get the matter of Mr. Merrick's estate cleared
up as soon as possible."

"Yes, ma'am. In a New York minute, as they say."
His tone was mocking.

She ignored it. "Is there a hotel here?"

"This is Hartley," he said testily. "Perico's up the
road a ways."

Andrea muttered a sound of frustration, thinking how

much she needed a shower and clean clothes. "It's getting late and I had hoped to meet with Mr. Merrick's lawyer today."

Blackburn scowled and climbed back into the truck, this time without holding the door for her. *Why is he so disagreeable?* Andrea wondered. *I'm the one who's been delayed, wrecked, and ruined today.*

When he spoke, Blackburn's tone was that of stifled impatience. "Well, I'm afraid ol' Merrick made me executor of his will. You'll be mostly dealin' with me for all your new wealth. I'll do my best though, ma'am," he added. Andrea thought the humility was tinged with sarcasm.

"I thought I'd take you right out to Mantilla Bluff and you can start sizing up the loot."

"Mr. Blackburn—"

"Prettiest little spread west of the Pecos. 'Course, you know it ain't really so little. Yes, ma'am, you're one lucky little lady to get the ranch, the grazing rights, the mineral rights . . . all for nothing." He gave her a knowing leer.

Was he really this big a rube or did he hate her as much as she hated him?

"Just a moment, Mr. Blackburn," she said. "I know our acquaintance has not begun well, but I resent your implication that I'm just here to collect, as you put it, my 'loot.' "

Blackburn turned to look at her. His shadowed eyes seemed to grow darker. The mocking edge was gone from his voice. "Why are you here, then?"

Andrea was incredulous. "Because you insisted!" she exploded, all the frustrations of her journey and the fatigue of the hard-working ballet season boiling out of her.

"Didn't I tell you there was some mistake about the

man's will? Didn't I say I couldn't possibly he meant to give the place to? Didn't I advise for his relatives? *Didn't I?*"

She didn't wait for a reply. "Weren't insisting that I was, in fact, the one and only you the one insisting that I had to come to the estate?

"And, of course, Nigel thought that was A nice little trip out West. Fresh air, sun relaxation, take care of this little business care of Boston," Andrea said resentfully fault too.

"By the way, Mr. Blackburn, I don't sounding quite so . . . rustic in our phon Does this insulting, country bumpkin ac or are you just rude?"

"Rude? Beg pardon, ma'am," he dra the one screaming at the top of my l who just pulled me outta the bar ditch

Blackburn was draped against the t boot propped up on the dusty dashboa his heel, and his strong thigh swaye

She turned away from his contem ticed the mechanics at the garage interest. She wanted to be as far a this character out of an old western of making her feel so uncharacteri as foolish.

"Yes, well, let's just go on," phone at the ranch?"

"Yes'm," he replied, sitting u ing last week too."

She threw him a sharp look,

ter. Everyone expected the daughter to follow in the mother's footsteps. And Andrea wanted nothing more desperately. She had always wanted it. Winning the role in "Giselle" and dancing it as beautifully as her mother could have danced it would be the realization of all her life's dreams.

Andrea wanted this role and feared it with equal fervor. She had to succeed to fulfill her parents' plans for her, yet she worried that she could never be as good a dancer as her mother. To fail would destroy Andrea, destroy her burgeoning career, and, worst of all, destroy the memory of the two beloved people who hadn't lived to see her recent successes.

She had always been a quiet, reserved person who seldom let anyone know her heart's turmoil. But when she heard about the opportunity at the Boston Ballet she became as animated and excited as any little ballerina at her first performance of "The Red Shoes."

She had spent hours at the library researching "Giselle" and every performance of it. She researched the Boston company and its personnel just as thoroughly. She talked incessantly about the role, played its music continually, and thought of little else. Andrea always applied complete concentration to whatever project she was engaged in, but even her work at the festival this summer became training and preparation for her bid in Boston.

Nigel was excited about the opportunity too. He had more confidence in her ability than she had and he always seemed to be right. It was his advice and guidance that had advanced her career since her parents' deaths. But even Nigel was overwhelmed by her nervous eagerness for the role.

That was why Nigel had encouraged her to visit Texas

when Mr. Blackburn had called. "It would be a good change of scene," he had said. "And it would get you out of the way until the contract is ready to sign."

He was like her father, intolerant of emotional display. "Self-indulgent," Nigel had called her nervous worry. She would telephone him tonight to see if he had heard from Boston. She really should be there herself.

She was startled out of her reverie by an animal standing by the road. It was still as a statue for a moment, then it bolted.

"What was that?" she asked, like a surprised child.

"Hmm? Antelope. Had a lot of them this year. There's a herd of about fifteen out at the ranch," he said.

"It's beautiful. The markings on its face were so striking." She turned to look for the animal. Blackburn gave her another of his cryptic looks from under his hat brim and smiled slightly.

Andrea sat up straighter and resumed her businesslike air. She began to notice details of the stark landscape. The pale grassland seemed to go on forever, with little to interrupt the seam of the horizon. Every few miles she saw a small cluster of gnarled trees or a lone windmill and water tank. Cattle were scattered across the pastures. At least she didn't have to ask what those were. He'd really ridicule her for that.

The sun had just dipped below the prairie when the truck finally began a curving descent into a valley. To her right a small stream lined with large trees wound toward a long, low ranch house and outbuildings. When the truck made the last curve toward the house, Andrea caught sight of a huge outcropping of white stone and gasped. The remaining sunset cast a golden orange spotlight on its craggy face.

"It certainly does look like a mantilla," she murmured.

"The stone seems to drape from the 'comb' at the top of the bluff. A magnificent, jeweled lace mantilla. Remarkable."

She gazed enraptured until she realized Blackburn was staring at her with a satisfied smile.

"Your timing is impeccable, Mr. Blackburn," she said as he parked beside the house. "You managed to arrive at the precise moment the bluff is at its most spectacular."

"You're just bound and determined not to enjoy any of this, aren't you?" he said tiredly. "Is it Yankee stubbornness? A city slicker's fear of anything in nature? Or the great artist's disdain for anything but herself?"

Blackburn reached past her, hoisted the veterinary supply box, and kicked the pickup door open in one motion. "I used to say Easterners were good, decent folk once you got 'em to slow down and think about something outside of themselves," he muttered on the way up to the house.

He yelled over his shoulder, "Leave the dang suitcase! I'll carry it in for you. My mama always taught me to treat a woman like a lady whether she acts like one or not!"

Andrea flushed with anger at his presumptuous attitude and kicked open the other door. She set her mouth, thinking of sharp retorts for that boor as she reached for her bags. She looked up at Mantilla Bluff again and stopped. Her hand was trembling. That magnificent crag, its hot sunset hues rapidly turning to cool purple twilight, was the one she had seen in long-ago dreams. Once again she felt weak with dread. She was always running in those dreams. But was she running to the bluff or away from it?

Chapter Two

Andrea barely noticed the dark, plump little woman who greeted her at the door. She glanced curiously and apprehensively past her into the ranch house. A single step led directly into the wide entryway. Thick stucco filled in the walls between massive ancient log posts. The ceiling was made of the same solid beams and the floor was polished stone. Beyond was a spacious room with windows comprising one wall.

She admired the tasteful Spanish furnishings. Many were obviously quality antiques. Handwoven curtains hung from wrought-iron rods. Massive wood and leather chairs invited relaxed conversation. The trendy western decor Andrea had seen in the East was a kitschy imitation of the real thing. After the shock of seeing Mantilla Bluff, she was relieved that nothing in the room seemed familiar.

" . . . clean, and then I fixed up the white bedroom for you 'cause I think it's prettiest," Mrs. Gonzales was saying proudly.

"The house looks very nice. You've done an excellent job," Andrea said, trying to remember what else the smiling woman had said. "I'm sure the estate will pay you if you'll just let me know your rate and how many hours, Mrs . . . uh . . . ?"

The smile shut off and Mrs. Gonzales stiffened. "My name is Esperanza Gonzales. I was just trying to make you feel welcome. You don't want me here, you just say so.'' She turned abruptly and led the way down the hall. ''This the living room.''

Andrea didn't understand why her offer for prompt payment had offended. She looked accusingly at Blackburn, who had returned from depositing her suitcase somewhere down the hall.

''Money always the first thing you people think about?'' he muttered and brushed past her.

''I offered to pay her for her work. How can that be insulting?'' she asked in a whisper.

''She's more than a maid, she's a friend,'' he snapped. ''People do for their neighbors out here, Miss Zanovya. Especially when there's been a death.''

Andrea sighed with embarrassment and frustration. She couldn't do anything right today. Everyone probably thought she had known Merrick and was grieving over the loss. She dreaded having to explain the situation again and again when she didn't understand it herself.

She followed along the hall. Opposite the windows in the living room was an open railing overlooking the dining room several feet below. An intricately carved pine table and sideboard showed the same Spanish influence as the rest of the house. Again there was no spark of recognition and Andrea was relieved. *How silly,* she thought. *I would remember a place as dramatic as this if I had been here before.*

Mrs. Gonzales was climbing the stairs. ''I think you will like the west side of the house so you can see La Mantilla *y los álamos*—the trees—and the creek and the front yard, too,'' she said as she showed Andrea a large white bedroom.

''Yes, it's very nice.'' Andrea knew to choose her next words carefully. ''I do appreciate all that you've done and I hope it won't be an imposition if I ask you for more help.''

Mrs. Gonzales brightened. Andrea was proud of her diplomacy.

"I suppose there are a million tasks in getting a house ready for sale,'' she said. "Could I rely on you as a friend of Mr. Merrick's to help me know how to dispose of things? You know, personal items? And books or things that his friends might like to have as keepsakes?''

The little woman nodded sadly and Andrea feared she had committed another small-town faux pas.

But Esperanza put her chubby arm around Andrea and gave her a warm squeeze. "You should stay here,'' she said quietly. "This should be your home.''

The gesture was so sweetly welcoming that Andrea nearly wept. She smiled down at her. "You're very kind, but I have a nice cramped little apartment and a big dance studio to call home. We could start work tomorrow if that would be convenient.''

"Oh, sí, we got lots of the old man's junk to clean out. He was such a pack rat.'' She shook her head in fond dismay. "You don't worry 'bout nothin' and rest tonight. I put two steaks on the grill already.''

"And they smell great.'' Blackburn's tall, powerful figure loomed in the bedroom doorway. He seemed massive, reaching past the short Hispanic woman to toss Andrea's garment bag on the bed. His rugged presence in the dainty room made Andrea strangely apprehensive.

"Why are there only two steaks? Aren't y'all staying?'' he asked.

"No, man, our new grandbabies are coming over tonight,'' Marcelino Gonzales said from behind him. As Blackburn turned, Andrea saw a stocky counterpart to Esperanza.

"Miss," he said, nodding a greeting to her. "Me and Espy, we got two new grandbabies. Twins! Both pretty girls."

"Congratulations," Andrea said, smiling.

"How's Max handling those two o'clock feedings, Espy?" Blackburn asked, winking slyly at her husband.

"Max! He don't get up at no two o'clock in the morning, Blackie." Esperanza slapped playfully at his muscular arm and began to shoo the men back down the hallway. "It's Lizzie who gets up with the babies all the time. My Max never even changed a diaper. I told Lizzie. . . . You come down to supper when you're ready, Miss," she said to Andrea as she left. "I told Lizzie to make him. He's not helpless."

Their words and laughter faded down the stairs. Andrea smiled at the warmth and friendliness she felt in the house. It was a place people were comfortable in. *Relax,* she admonished herself. These people were more casual and informal than she was used to. Hadn't Nigel warned her that things move more slowly in "the provinces," as he called it? *Be patient, you'll see the lawyer tomorrow and clear this matter up.* He would know more about Merrick's affairs than the hired hand.

The hired hand. She was even starting to think in rustic terms.

Andrea rummaged through her luggage for a comfortable change of clothes. She wanted to get out of her dirty, ragged state and put herself back together. She could deal with her surroundings and companions much better then. *I am very glad to be out of a moving vehicle,* she thought. *And I'm very, very hungry.*

She peeled off her traveling clothes and started brushing her hair. She heard their voices below her window, then doors slamming and a truck driving off. The house seemed lonely and still now. Andrea realized she was more alone than she had ever been in her life. Not only physically removed from the people and cities she knew and from any people on this isolated ranch, but alone in her responsibility for this inheritance and alone in the career move she wanted to make.

Her life and career had always proceeded naturally from season to season and dance company to company in logical progression as her abilities grew. Now she was attempting to take a major step forward, and she didn't possess the confidence she always assumed she would have at this point. This brief trip was the first instance she'd had time to really think about the changes coming if she landed that important role—and to face the fears of what would happen to her if she didn't.

Then she heard a screen door bang and someone whistling. Blackburn was still here. Even with the distance of a flight of stairs between them Andrea felt like he was too close. The same prickling sensations she'd felt sitting by him in the truck unnerved her now. She looked out the window and watched Blackburn turn the steaks on the grill. Just as she began to wish he'd left too, Blackburn glanced up. She quickly shrank back, knowing the filmy, ruffled curtains weren't much of a barrier. That was it, she realized—he made her feel he could always see through her. His gaze was sharp and penetrating even when she couldn't see his eyes from under the brim of that grubby hat.

She washed hurriedly to scrub herself free of that irrational thought and slipped into a pair of comfortable knit slacks. The hired hand, she thought again, remembering the way his firm thighs rippled in his jeans when he walked. She recalled noticing precisely how broad his shoulders were when they rode in the crowded pickup and how rough his hand was when he shifted the gears and brushed against her. She felt a sudden warmth in her face.

I'm blushing, Andrea realized, appalled. She jerked a loose sweater over her head and angrily crammed her feet into her shoes. *Really, you're not some silly, boy-crazy teenager,* she scolded herself. As if to prove the point, she pulled her long, loose auburn hair back and wrapped a tight band around it.

Blackburn rinsed the lather off his face, arms, and chest as best he could in the kitchen sink. It felt so refreshing after his long, tiring day of ranch work that he decided to duck his whole head in the cool water. The wave of cold seeping through his hair and over his scalp calmed the rising irritation he was feeling with that woman. She was just as rude and self-absorbed as he had expected.

He straightened and shook his wet hair like a dog coming out of a pond and wiped his face with a tiny kitchen towel. He'd been painfully aware of his scruffy appearance ever since Miss Zanovya had given him a disparaging once-over when she first saw him. He could tell what she thought about him and her attitude angered him. What's worse, her opinion seemed to matter to him.

Yeah, he reminded himself, he knew exactly what women like that thought of his kind. He'd had enough experience with Yankee women to know they only valued men for their expensive possessions, high-powered jobs, and impressive connections. He'd lived in that world long enough to get his fill of snobbish women. Even Helen had. . . . He stopped the memory and forced it away. He had other concerns now.

Miss Grand-and-Glorious Andrea Zanovya. In all these years, she'd never had time or thought for Dolf Merrick.

Even after the old man died and left her everything, she couldn't be bothered to come to Texas. Blackburn had to cajole, connive, and insist to get her here. And everything he'd heard out of her since was a whine or a complaint or some kind of fool remark. Miss High and Mighty trying to . . .

Well, really, he remembered, she was kind of funny trying to pull that mesquite. Dancing around in the sand barefooted, then boom, right down on her cute little rear.

Blackburn shook his wet head again, chasing that memory away. He ran his fingers through his hair to push it out of his face and found a clean shirt in the laundry room. He guessed he'd have to get all his stuff out of the house now that she was here. He didn't even remember what he'd left at the old man's place over the course of several years of being neighbor, volunteer ranch hand, and friend. Merrick was a fine old boy, Blackburn thought. He deserved better than this.

Blackburn was just taking the steaks off the grill when he looked through the kitchen windows and saw her gliding down the stairs. She had looked plenty sexy in her rumpled dress and torn stockings but she looked even better in soft, casual clothes. Long and lean like a cat, he thought. Graceful, elegant . . . and deadly, he added with an inner sigh.

"Out here," he called to her through the open door. "Hope you like 'em well done. You better. It's a law in Texas.

"Get the salad out of the icebox and whatever else you want. Table's set out here."

Andrea brought out a large salad bowl and a pie piled with a mound of meringue, set them down on the wrought-iron table, and watched him serve large steaks and potatoes from the grill. She didn't make eye contact, he noted. He'd wait and let her take the lead, he decided.

"It's kind of you to do this, but if you have other things to do please don't feel you have to stay," she said stiffly. "I mean after you have your dinner, of course."

"Thank you, ma'am. I'd like a night off," he said. Her snooty manner riled him so much he couldn't help taunting her. "You want me to eat in the kitchen?"

She flashed an angry look. "I didn't mean to sound condescending. I just didn't want you to be inconvenienced. You must have . . . things to do . . . elsewhere. I'll be fine here alone."

"I'll get out of your way in a little while." He held her chair for her, then sat across from her.

She started to say something, but didn't. Blackburn watched her face as the changing twilight ceded to patio lanterns. Her slender, pale features were delicately lovely. He wondered what she was like when she was happy and relaxed, if she ever was. Right now she looked like a worried child, he thought. There was something gnawing at her.

"Mr. Blackburn, who would you say was Mr. Merrick's closest friend?"

"Me."

"Of course. Had you known him long?"

"All my life. My place is south of here."

"Your place?"

He liked the way she looked when there were questions in her eyes. "My ranch," he said gruffly, sawing at his steak to remind himself what she was.

"Oh, you have a ranch too?" She seemed to be trying to sort something out in her mind. "I thought you worked for Mr. Merrick."

"I did, now and again. I tried to do all the heavy stuff

for him these last few years after he got down in his back, but the old goat was hard to get ahead of,'' Blackburn said. He could still see the old man struggling with a bale of hay he no longer had the strength to lift. ''He was determined to work till he died. . . . Guess he did.''

He wondered how much more he should tell her.

''You're sure Mr. Merrick had no one else to whom he could have left the ranch?'' she asked, frowning.

''Guess not.'' He couldn't keep the bitterness out of his voice.

Her clear gray eyes looked at him worriedly. He concentrated on his plate. He wasn't going to get into the whole thing right now. And he wasn't going to let her rattle him. The pleasure of telling Miss Andrea Zanovya exactly what he thought of her would have to wait until he was finished with his task.

He forced his voice back to the proper tone. ''The old codger had nobody for as long as I can remember. Lots of good friends, but no real family. Should have. He was a good old man.''

''Pity,'' she said simply. Her polite lack of interest infuriated him. He clenched his jaw and looked out across the peaceful horizon in an effort to control his temper.

''What about charities or organizations that were important to him?'' she went on.

''Well, that would be hard to narrow down,'' he said. ''He cared about a lot of things and had several projects going.''

Was she really trying to find someone to give the ranch to? Or tax shelters? Or was she preempting possible challenges to the will? *Yeah, she's like a cat,* he thought again. *Hard to figure.*

After a silence Andrea said, ''Mr. and Mrs. Gonzales seem very nice. Capable.''

"But Blackie, they've got to get the meat started tomorrow," KittyLu protested, shaking her head in exasperation. "See why I should've met Miss Zanovya at the airport? I could've told her everything by now."

Blackburn raised his eyebrows and muttered something under his breath. Andrea tried to get back in the conversation before KittyLu took off again. "Mrs. Lawler, I—"

"Land sakes, Mrs. Lawler's my mother-in-law. Call me KittyLu. We had the plans all made when Dolf passed over. 'Course, we didn't know if we ought to go ahead or not, so soon." KittyLu looked sadly at her coffee. "But we decided it really would be kinda nice to keep up the tradition. Now, don't you worry about a bit of it. Everybody pitches in and—"

"Wait. Wait." Andrea held up a hand to stop her. "What are you talking about?"

Flustered, KittyLu blinked and looked from face to face. "Oh, well, we . . . "

Blackburn explained, "All the folks around, the whole community, always has an annual barbecue here at Mantilla Bluff the third Saturday of August."

"It's potluck," KittyLu added. "We talked about moving it somewhere else, but we thought it would be nice to have it here one more time, for old Dolf. He started the tradition and he loved having folks over. You'd like to keep it going in his memory, wouldn't you?" She looked pleadingly at Andrea.

"I'm sorry, but I'm not in a position to entertain a large group like that. I must shut up the house and get back East as soon as possible," Andrea said.

KittyLu frowned and blinked a few times while she thought. "Well, can't be helped, I guess," she said quietly. "I've been coming to these barbecues since I can remember. Makes me feel so old to think. . . .

"But, now don't you feel bad." Sniffing and shaking her head, she patted Andrea's hand. "I understand. We'll just move it to the Carswells' like we talked about."

Andrea saw her disappointment and felt a little guilty for causing it. KittyLu was such a silly, childlike woman Andrea instinctively wanted to please her. She looked to Blackburn to help her explain but he was scowling and thinking hard about something. "I'm sorry," she said, edging toward the door and hoping the others would take her hint. "I'm pressed for time, you see."

"Oh, of course," KittyLu agreed. "Are you dancing in New York or Pittsburgh again this season?"

Andrea was surprised that the woman knew anything about her career moves and it must have showed in her expression.

"Hon, you're famous in Perico," KittyLu said. "Everyone knows about the grand ballet star that old Dolf Merrick left his whole place to."

Andrea stammered for a reply.

"Don't be mad," KittyLu said. "Everybody knows everybody else's business in a small town. We're all dyin' to get to know you. You'll find some of the old folks remember your mama. My mama was so fond of her."

Andrea was astounded. "My mother?" Then Merrick must have known her mother somehow, she thought. It had been a casual acquaintance, since he had never been mentioned. And it didn't explain why he made Andrea his heir. She had already decided that Merrick must have been an eccentric. But since he apparently was highly esteemed by his many friends here, why didn't one of *them* inherit?

The whole thing made Andrea increasingly uneasy. She

wished she had never come to Texas. If only she'd just tossed the letters in the trash and refused all calls from Blackburn. She looked up to see him staring at her as if he read her thoughts. And from the scowl of contempt, it was apparent he disapproved. She frowned back at him.

"'Course, you'll meet most of them at the barbecue," KittyLu was saying. "You will come over to the Carswell place for it, won't you? I hope they can get a new pit dug without any trouble and I've got to remember the flowers. What will you be dancing this year?"

KittyLu's random switches of conversation made Andrea dizzy. This time the woman paused for an answer. "Uh, I . . . I hope to be dancing 'Giselle' with the Boston Ballet," Andrea said. "Plans are not finalized, however. That's why I'll be going as soon as I make some sort of arrangement for the property."

Blackburn slammed his coffee mug down on the counter, turning his back to the women. KittyLu eyed him worriedly.

"Well, we were all hoping that you'd take up residence at Mantilla Bluff," she said, "but, of course, we understand that you have a busy career back East and might not be able to spend much time here right now.

"We each have to do what we have to do, don't we?" she added, with a warning look at Blackburn as he turned toward them again. "Judge not, lest ye be judged, my mama would say."

Andrea wondered what was being said between the lines of KittyLu's words. Blackburn was in a perpetual state of grumpiness and disapproval, she had already decided, but KittyLu was sending him some sort of message apparently related to a previous conversation about her. Andrea didn't like strangers knowing more about her activities than she intended, not even this good-natured busybody.

"Yes," she said crisply, "you're quite right. And as I said, I *am* pressed for time." She walked to the door, pointedly showing her out.

KittyLu looked surprised for a moment but quickly recovered her composure and gathered her purse, keys, and empty grocery sacks. She gave Blackburn an affectionate squeeze and said to Andrea, "Now I know Blackie will take good care of you, but if there's anything at all any of the rest of us can do, you just holler." She patted Andrea reassuringly again and swept out, her accoutrements jingling and clanging with every movement.

"Come on, sweeties," she shouted to the little girls who had stopped clearing away the dishes to play on the patio. "Tell Miss Zanovya you're pleased to meet her."

"Pleased to meet you," they chorused in unison and waved.

Their departure was like the sudden stillness after a storm. Andrea waited a moment before she turned back into the kitchen where Blackburn leaned against the counter. Andrea noticed how very tired he looked.

"I told you she was an experience, didn't I?" he asked with a weary smile.

"An experience I'll never forget," she agreed. "I'm glad you explained the term 'funeral food,' I was worried."

Blackburn chuckled. "I could tell."

There was an awkward silence. Andrea felt more comfortable around him when they were arguing. These periods of truce were unnerving. She glanced out the screen door again. The bluff was a hulking mass in the darkness. She thought of Blackburn's strong hands gripping her

shoulders when he tried to kiss her. She had a panicky
urge to run out the door away from him.

"I need to explain several areas of ranch operation
before you make any decision," he said. "In as much
detail as you'll allow."

"Of course. I know you take your responsibility for
the estate seriously, but all that can wait until tomorrow,"
she said. "I'm rather tired and I know you've had a busy
day. Baby cows and stranded cars and all." She tried to
smile.

"Yeah. Okay."

He studied her for a moment, his gaze seeming to bore
right through her. What a commanding stage presence he
would have, Andrea thought.

As he stalked past her she sidled away so he wouldn't
get too close. Halfway out the door he stopped. "Sorry
about . . . uh . . . out there," he said. "Didn't mean any
harm."

Andrea watched him stride across the patio, pick up
his hat from a chair, slap it against his knee, and cram
it down on his head. So that was a roughriding he-man,
she thought, smiling at her earlier musings. It was quite
a concept.

After his truck had driven out of sight Andrea listened
to the eerie silence of the house. The lateness of the hour,
her fatigue, and the remoteness of the ranch left her feeling like she'd been marooned on a distant, lonely planet.
The personality of the old man seemed to hover nearby.
Not simply a house with unfamiliar furnishings, it was a
comfortable home that someone had recently left behind
forever.

To chase away the spooky mood Andrea busied herself
clearing away the dinner things the little girls had missed
and closing the house for the night. The clatter and work

relaxed her, then a few stretching exercises helped ease the tension of the flight and the rest of the day's activities out of her muscles.

She wandered through the quiet house, her steps echoing softly in the emptiness. She was relieved to be by herself at last and she was curious about the house and the man who had lived here. The kitchen was tidy and well organized, probably because of Esperanza's attention, Andrea decided. But the activities and habits of the old man were evident in other rooms. On the antique sideboard in the dining room, leather work gloves lay next to a chipped china candy dish holding a few hard candies, several loose keys, a tangle of rubber bands, and some canceled stamps torn from the corners of envelopes. There was also a packet of small rolling papers and a muslin drawstring bag labeled "Bull Durham." *I don't believe this,* Andrea thought, pulling open the drawstring and peeking at the contents. He actually made his own cigarettes. *That I would like to have seen.*

Who was this Adolf Merrick, anyway? she wondered. Why did he leave her what was, if Blackburn was right about what he said, vast and valuable holdings?

She glanced at the hats hanging on the hall tree and the boots tossed in the corner of the entryway. It looked as if the owner were expected to return for them soon, she thought with a shudder.

As she entered the spacious living room she admired its feeling of comfort again. Andrea even thought she could smell the richness of the leather furniture, lingering tobacco, and perhaps a trace of wood smoke. There was something else too. She couldn't quite name it, but it was something green and fresh-scented. She stopped at the ceiling-high bookcase beside the large hearth. It held a haphazard collection of cheap paperbacks, quality hardbacks, and tattered magazines. She read titles from Dickens to Louis L'Amour.

"Dorothy Parker, as well? You certainly had eclectic taste in reading matter, Mr. Merrick," she mused as she picked up scattered items. *Farm Journal* and *Dance* magazine.

It was the issue with that great photo of her, she realized. She flipped through it. Page 24 was missing. It looked like it had been carefully cut out. Why?

Andrea put the magazine down and shivered as if she were being watched. He could have been a ballet aficionado, even way out here, she thought. He was obviously eccentric. Or crazy.

Blackburn, help me, she pleaded silently. Andrea wished he were still there going through the rooms with her, describing the significance of each item and telling her about the old man. Somehow she knew Blackburn could explain her role in this affair, if only he would.

But why did she want him back now, she wondered, when she had been desperately eager for him to leave earlier? When he was here she had a strong physical urge to shove him out of the room. When he was gone she sought the shelter of his powerful bulk. How could he make her feel so protected and so threatened all at once?

Andrea suddenly longed to be with Nigel. He was her source of strength in confusing times. She hurried to the telephone at the end of the hallway and dialed Nigel's number. She sat on the stair step to wait for his answer and looked around. *How did I know the phone was in this little nook back here?* she thought with a start. *I saw it earlier. I must have.* She leaned wearily against the newel post. It was cool against her cheek. *Pick up,* she urged the buzzing phone. *It's time for my reality check.*

Finally there was a click and Nigel's crisp "Hello?"

"Hello, Nigel, it's me."

"Andrea, darling, how is the heiress?" he crooned too dramatically, emphasizing the second syllable of her name. "Have you settled things with the lawyer?"

"Not yet. It's been very frustrating. I had trouble just getting in from—" she began.

Nigel broke in. "I talked to Howard and I'm all set in the road manager post. This is the beginning of my management career!"

"Congratulations, dear," she said. "We knew they would hire you. How could they not? You're the best."

This felt right, normal. If she were back in New York they would be with friends toasting his new career and she would have that familiar feeling of security and stability. "I wish I could be there with you to celebrate," she added.

"I've started doing my networking, contacting people I know all along the tour route who might be of any use. I go on staff at the first of the month," Nigel said. Andrea realized Nigel's voice always sounded slightly irritated and impatient.

"This is just wonderful, Nigel dear," she said. "Of course, we knew this would work out just the way you wanted. Howard practically promised last spring—"

"Listen, 'Drea," he went on, "I'm going over to Boston to find an apartment, check out my office, and look over the schedule, so I won't be here when you return. But please don't forget to call Margo about those tapes, will you?"

"Yes, of course, I will. Nigel dear, has Howard said anything about my contract?" she asked.

"Not to me, but then, I really didn't ask him," Nigel said offhandedly. "Why don't you call him yourself? Or buttonhole him at the Vandergriff party?"

Andrea was irked at his cool attitude. "Nigel, how can you be so casual about this? Darling, we've known since April that you would get your job. I'm the one on tenterhooks! I'm the one who's really had to compete for a principle slot with the Boston company."

"Yes, yes, I know. The breakout role of a lifetime; dance it for dear old mommy and all that," he said impatiently. "You've certainly reminded me of it often enough."

His words stung her. "I'm sorry, I didn't realize my goals and aspirations had made me such a bore," she retorted angrily.

"Don't be ridiculous," he said in the same dismissive tone she had used with Blackburn when she said the words. Nigel was always detached in his dealings with her, she realized. And self-centered, she admitted. Why did it bother her now, when it never had before?

They had always moved in tandem as partners without really becoming a couple. They shared the world of ballet and that was enough. She didn't feel quite so alone and Nigel didn't require a great deal of emotional commitment. She could keep her dreams and her fears to herself.

"Why do you always get so emotional about things?" he went on. "I thought this little Texas excursion was supposed to help you relax."

"That was your idea, but this little Texas excursion has been anything but relaxing. I wrecked my car, probably ruined my suit, the people are unbelievable," Andrea said. "And this ranch, this is going to be more complicated—"

"Well, there's nothing I can do to help you with it, Andrea. I have too much to think about here."

"I'm not asking you to do anything," she said. "I was simply trying to discuss my day."

"I'm sure you're very tired," he said evenly. "Get some rest and I'll see you in a few days."

Andrea sighed and ran her hand through her hair. "Yes, well, good night," she said. "And congratulations on your good news."

There was a silent pause, then Nigel said, "Listen, don't worry about your career. If you don't get Boston, you can go back to the Pittsburgh company, as always."

"You haven't understood at all, have you?" she snapped. "You truly don't know how I feel about any of this, do you? This is my defining moment, Nigel. Getting this role determines my career. It determines my life! Can't you care about that?"

"You're worried about us, aren't you?" he asked. "So don't go back to Pittsburgh. You can come to Boston with me whether you get the part or not. Is that what you wanted to hear?"

"No, that's not what I wanted to hear."

"Andrea, I hate it when you get needy. Look, we'll . . . be together . . . whether you go to Pittsburgh or Boston or stay in New York or whatever happens," Nigel said. "You can dance or teach or just live off your inheritance. Don't worry about us."

"I won't," Andrea said simply. She had given up trying to make him understand.

"Have fun, babe," Nigel said. "See you soon."

She put down the phone but did not rise from the step where she sat. "Maybe you will and maybe you won't, you conceited, self-absorbed, thickheaded male!"

Why were they all so stupid and so sure of their tremendous importance? Andrea felt gloomier and more alone than before. She had often been alone in her life. Even in the groups of students and then professional dancers she had spent her time with, there was always a feeling of isolation. It was necessary for the concentration that her mother and father had taught her was required of a good dancer. That was why all her friends were dancers. They understood one another and the life-style. Outsiders had to learn to take second place behind the long hours of daily classes and rehearsals.

She had never regretted this life. With the nomadic nature of professional ballet, she had acquaintances all over the country and over much of Europe. Acquaintances, contacts, and, yes, some true friends. Until now that had been sufficient. Until now even Nigel's remoteness had been enough.

But now she needed more. She needed the role she had spent so many years preparing for and she needed Nigel to understand that.

What if she didn't get it? She faced the question seriously for the first time. Could she go back to Pittsburgh? Would it be enough to continue her career in important but secondary roles? Could she live without stardom? Of course, Andrea knew the answer immediately. She wasn't vain and it wasn't fame she was after. It was fulfilling the dream her parents had for her that was driving her.

Could she teach somewhere? Many dancers turned to teaching after their stage careers were over. She had always enjoyed children and teaching, but would that satisfy her if she had never reached her own goals?

She didn't ask herself if she would go to Boston with Nigel if she didn't get "Giselle." The idea was unthinkable. Without dance her life would have no purpose. Even a life with Nigel.

Andrea shivered. *I care deeply for Nigel,* she reasoned. *Of course I do.* But she realized that she had never thought of him except as part of her dancer's world. Would she love Nigel enough just as a husband and not as her partner in a pas de deux? She pushed the thought away.

I'll get the part, she told herself, rising determinedly from the step. *I have to.*

Chapter Four

The quiet country night kept Andrea awake for a long while and staring out the window at the bluff, white and silent in the moonlight. She remembered the first startling sight she'd had of it, burning golden in the sunset. She also remembered the first frightening moment she'd seen Blackburn. And then how he looked at dinner with his wet hair curling on his forehead. It had dripped on his shirt and he'd been too busy watching her to notice. It made her nervous when he paid such close attention to her, even more than when he ignored her.

She thought of the tingle of awkward embarrassment she'd felt when she climbed through the fence and brushed against him. She remembered sitting so close to his muscled shoulders in the truck that she could almost feel their strength. She remembered the power of his embrace on the patio and the warmth of his lips approaching hers. She had yearned to complete the kiss and press against his hard chest, perhaps feel his hands in her hair and the scratch of his late-day beard on her neck.

Telling herself she was having hallucinations caused by the thin air of the Texas high plains, Andrea flipped to her other side, punched up her pillows, and finally fell asleep by imagining traffic noise beneath her window.

She awoke surprisingly well rested and cheered by the bright sunshine streaming into the room. She decided that if she kept that cheerful attitude and a positive focus on estate business she could make up for the disasters of the day before and finish what she'd come here for. And get back to her normal life.

She would let Blackburn spend a few hours explaining the affairs of the ranch and behave as though she understood everything completely. She would listen thoughtfully to his advice, thank him profusely, then instruct him to close the house and sell out. She could be back on a plane to New York tonight or early tomorrow.

No more of this inheritance mystery. No more disturbance of her well-planned life. No more confusion in her feelings toward that man, she thought happily as she dressed in jeans and a light knit top. She brushed her hair vigorously and let it hang loose around her shoulders. She was beginning to feel as though she were on vacation. No, it was more like she was comfortably back to work. *That's it,* she thought. She could handle this matter the same way she danced. Know the choreography, relax, stay in control, and focus the energy.

The railing overlooking the dining room would do for her barre exercises, she decided. It was a bit too low, but then her jeans were a bit too tight. It was invigorating to do her routine workout again after a day of airplane and car rides.

Esperanza and two of her daughters had arrived early and were clattering around in the back of the house sorting and packing.

"I really appreciate your doing all this, Mrs. Gonzales," Andrea called to her again as she lifted one toe toward the ceiling and pressed her forehead on the opposite knee. "I'm going to rely completely on your judgment about the household things, if that's all right."

She was in inexplicably high spirits this morning. A

determination to get her business accomplished today, she guessed.

"What you doing, Miss?" Espy gazed up from the dining room.

"Grande plié." Andrea said, curving her arm gracefully over her head.

"Oh, sí."

"A dancer has to do a full warm-up every day to get her muscles ready for movement. To avoid strain and injury," she explained. "Of course, I won't have rehearsal for a week or two but I need to exercise so I won't get creaky." She looked up but Espy had returned to her tasks. Andrea smiled. Few people understood the hours of careful conditioning a dancer's body needed.

When she finished stretching she joined the older woman in the kitchen. "I assume Mr. Blackburn will arrive to discuss business soon, but I'm at your service until then," Andrea said.

"No, no, you have business to do. My girls can do this and we'll leave his desk papers and stuff for you to look at," Espy said.

"Oh, all right. That sounds like a good plan," Andrea said uncertainly. She wasn't eager to begin her day by going through Merrick's personal papers. "I think I'll take a quick jog first. You know, take advantage of this smogless air."

The air was clean and crisp. The sun was warm except when an occasional breeze stirred the cool prairie morning. Andrea loped slowly around the base of Mantilla Bluff and up to the high ground behind it. The thing was just as huge and foreboding in the sunshine, she thought. On the far side the land sloped gently for a few hundred yards to a small, azure lake. She jogged down to it and stopped to catch her breath at the water's edge, wondering if it was possible to swim in the crystal pool. She looked beyond it and saw some kind of machine or collection of metallic parts.

An ancient, topless Jeep roared before a cloud of dust toward her. Blackburn was driving.

"Good morning," she called to him and waved. The vehicle creaked to a stop beside her. Blackburn was wearing what Andrea guessed was a "before" version of yesterday's attire—a less-battered straw hat, faded but crisply clean jeans, and a pale blue plaid western shirt without the rips. It still pulled disturbingly taut across the muscles of his chest, she noticed.

"I know I'm a city slicker and all," she said, "but what in the world are those silver pipe contraptions over there?" She tried to be as bright and cheery as she could. Today she would be a model of cooperation and confidence. And beat him at his own game in the process.

He pushed his hat back an inch and eyed her cautiously. "Mornin'. You trying to run all the way back to New York?"

"No, no." She laughed. "Just filling my lungs with pure Texas air. And you?" She leaned casually on the opposite side of the Jeep.

"Just keeping an eye on things. The Gonzales boys are leasing some rangeland from you. You'll see them around too, probably. I figured you'd want us to keep things going for you a while. Merrick's horses are over at my place if you want to ride any time." He jerked his head to indicate the direction from which he'd come.

"I really appreciate all the trouble you're taking for me," she said graciously. "You must take a management fee from the estate. Unless, of course, you already do."

A moment of stony silence passed. His eyes narrowed and he took on the same tired, disappointed expression he had worn yesterday. He switched his gaze to the horizon. It seemed very far away.

"Oops, my New York is showing again, isn't it? 'Folks do for one another out here,' " she quoted him and laughed. She knew her wide smile could be sweetly engaging and hard to resist. It worked. His expression softened.

"But, honestly, this must take away time from your law practice," she continued.

"Not much."

She climbed into the Jeep. "Well, in that case, you promised to show me Mantilla Bluff and environs. Now, what are those things?" She pointed to the pipes she had asked about.

"Those are some of the CO2 wells." He gunned the engine and they lurched off.

"Those? Really? How do they work?" She intended to be fascinated by everything today.

"There on the left is the wellhead. Most of what you see are gathering lines. They lead to the compressor down that way, see?"

"Yes, I see."

They bounced across the rough pasture and over small rises in the nearly flat landscape. The crisp morning breeze stung her cheeks slightly. Andrea threw her head back, letting the wind tangle her hair, enjoying the sensations. She felt so vital and free in this vast, open terrain. She didn't even feel intimidated by Blackburn's presence today. It must be a reaction to the uncluttered space of the prairie, she thought. And her determination to regain control of her life.

Blackburn observed her with quick sidelong glances. It seemed he was constantly assessing her actions and motives. Andrea wondered why. Merrick had been his friend, of course, but was that sufficient reason for him to care so much about the character of this stranger who inherited his ranch?

"This is fascinating," she said loudly, gripping the seat. It was difficult to talk while the Jeep jolted. "I had no idea they pumped carbon dioxide out of the ground. I thought we were trying to get rid of carbon dioxide in the environment."

Andrea wished she could think of an intelligent question to ask about the process. "So what do they do with it?"

Blackburn laughed. "Ask the folks at Coca-Cola."

She couldn't tell if he was mocking her again or not, but she was determined to remain pleasant.

"Do they really use it for fizzing up soft drinks?" she asked.

He nodded. "And for everything from dry ice to liquid refrigerant used in plastic manufacturing to 'cold testing' missile components to freezing the liquid centers of golf balls for winding to making aspirin."

"Oh, stop. Okay, maybe I'll believe all that manufacturing stuff," she protested, "but aspirin?"

"Well, I don't know much about aspirin," he replied. "I never got headaches—until yesterday."

She frowned teasingly at his joke and Blackburn turned the Jeep sharply to the right. They seemed to fly over the rough ground, Andrea's hair whipping in her face. They careened over a deep rut, nearly flinging Andrea out of the doorless vehicle. She squealed and instinctively clutched his arm.

He looked down at her and smiled. "Hold on." Andrea was aware of deep brown eyes, glints of sun making his hair seem lighter, and the warm hard muscles of the arm she clung to. She had the same lost, suspended feeling she'd had last night when he was about to kiss her.

"Now what do we do?" she asked. "Uh, I mean . . ." Had that sounded flirtatious? She looked away and quickly settled back into her seat. *Oh, please, don't blush,* she ordered herself.

They stopped and he said, "Open the gate." She couldn't look at him but she could tell by the tone that he was grinning at her.

She smoothed her hair and walked self-consciously to the gate. She had to search for a moment before finding the sliding latch. She awkwardly shoved it open. He drove the Jeep through and stopped a few yards away, waiting for her to catch up. It was another small struggle to get the heavy gate latched again, then she ran to jump in beside him.

"You're slow but you might make a good hand one day," Blackburn said.

She arched an eyebrow. "We aim to please."

"Ouch," he said with a small chuckle. When they stopped at the edge of a creek he leaned forward and searched for a crossing. He pressed the gas pedal and veered left. The old Jeep crashed through the water, splashing Andrea with large, cold drops.

She shrieked again. "You did that intentionally!"

His laugh rang out deep and masculine. Andrea liked the sound and liked that she had caused it, but she wasn't sure she liked this heart-pounding breathlessness she felt. *It's the cold water,* she told herself.

The vehicle lurched to a stop and there was sudden silence. She pushed her windblown hair back and listened to the sounds of the prairie. A few distant birds twittered and there was just a whisper of wind in the grass.

"About ten percent of these are yours," he said, indicating the black cattle grazing. He climbed out and approached one particularly large animal. "We'll have some more calves before winter," he said, slapping it affectionately on its broad belly.

"Okay," Andrea said nervously.

He turned to grin at her again. "Come take a look," he invited.

"I can see perfectly well from here."

"You're not afraid of a little ol' mama Chianina, are you?" He stroked the smooth black hide, then guided the animal closer to the Jeep. "She's just a big, fat baby herself."

"Yes, very big. Can't it just stay over there?"

He laughed again. She liked that laugh. It was so loose and free, so masculine and lusty. He slapped the cow's rump and she trotted off a few steps and bent her head to munch grass. Andrea watched Blackburn survey the pasture and climb back in the vehicle. He was perfectly suited to this scene, she thought—his rugged face tanned by days in the sun, his arms muscled by the hard physical labor, the love of the land apparent in his eyes. She wanted to say something to him, but she didn't know what.

"What?" he questioned as he climbed back in the Jeep. "You were getting ready to say something."

"Just . . . well, you looked like I feel when I'm on-stage." She knew that didn't make sense.

"Great. I always wanted to look like a little tippy-toe dancer," he said with a snarl.

Now Andrea laughed at him. "Never mind."

They drove randomly around the ranch for a while. She didn't want to interrupt his concentration. It was enough for her to observe his care for the land and the occasional cluster of grazing cattle. She couldn't guess why she found it so relaxing, so serene—no, she was never really comfortable around him. Being with him this morning was exciting, adventurous in a strange way.

It was no longer an effort to be fascinated by everything she saw. She asked about each kind of plant she saw, what was involved in caring for the cattle and horses, and, finally, just how far away the ranch boundaries were, anyway. It seemed like they had wandered miles from the ranch house. Andrea recalled his cryptic comment, "a million miles and yesterdays." This place and this day were a million miles from her other life.

Coming to a vast, planted field Andrea smiled delight-edly and said, "Oh, real American amber waves of grain!"

"Do you want to get out of the Jeep and look at this? Or do wheat stalks scare you too?" he teased.

"This I can deal with."

She followed him to the fence. He easily swung his long legs over it but turned and stretched a gap in the wires for her to crawl through. One side of his mouth curved slightly in a smirk and his eyes challenged her. Andrea was mortified. He was deliberately reminding her of her embarrassment of yesterday. She knew she'd blush and stammer unforgivably if she didn't think of something quickly.

She met his gaze defiantly, sauntered slowly to the fence, then nimbly jumped over the top wire and landed lightly beside him. She looked up at him in triumph.

"Too bad you didn't try that the first time." His voice was a gentle murmur near her ear.

"Yes, it would have prevented a lot of trouble." She hadn't meant to match his tone.

She hadn't meant to stroke his chest either. Really, she was just trying to steady herself, but when he released the fence wires he had her in his embrace. She didn't know what she could do or say to salvage the situation without embarrassment.

He ran his fingers through her hair, pushing it off her face. "You're a mess," he said. It sounded like a compliment.

Andrea knew he was going to kiss her and knew she was going to love it, but instead Blackburn clenched his jaw and turned away. Well, that was probably for the best, she thought, letting out her breath and feeling disappointed anyway. He frowned slightly and strode to the nearest wheat stalk, roughly pulling a red, ripe head of grain.

He showed her how to roll it between her hands to separate the kernels from the chaff. "Here, taste it." He popped some in his mouth and held out the rest for her.

"Just like that, without washing it?" she asked, skeptically eyeing the little brownish-red pellets in his hand.

"It's been washed in the rain and the wind."

He munched the grain. "Needs more sun. About a week, at least. Sure you don't want to try it?"

"No, no, I never eat un-sunned wheat."

"Sissy."

"Oh, all right." She popped some in her mouth and grimaced as she tried to chew the hard kernels. They had a nutty, dusty flavor and Andrea wondered how he could possibly judge their maturity from this. But she agreed. "Yes, definitely a week of sun. Eight or nine days, perhaps."

"Used to boil this up for coffee. I'll fix you some sometime."

"Really, Blackburn, I don't believe that for a minute. How gullible do you think I am?"

His hearty laughter rang out. It was wonderfully virile and sent a shiver through her.

"Ready to cross the creek again?" he asked and winked at her. They jumped back to the other side of the fence.

"Haven't you heard about that terrific new invention? It's called a bridge. If I knew the way I'd just walk back to the house," she snapped.

"You mean I could just leave you here and you'd have no idea how to get home?" he asked. He quickened his pace.

"Blackburn! You wouldn't dare!"

They raced, laughing, to the Jeep. She reached it just as he leaped into the driver's seat. He seemed surprised that she could keep up with him so easily. "Guess you do a lot of running and jumping," he said, letting his gaze wander slowly down her legs. She knew she should rebuff such open appreciation of her form, but she was rather enjoying it.

She climbed in beside him, marveling at her feeling of exhilaration. It was as if she were in some kind of Never Never Land alone with him far from the rest of the world. They sat for a moment trying to catch their breaths and admiring the landscape. Andrea delighted in every sight and sensation.

"This place is truly beautiful, Mr. Blackburn," she said.

He put his arm on the seat behind her. "My friends call me Blackie," he said softly. He leaned down to her.

"Don't be ridiculous," she whispered, relaxing into his embrace.

"Hmm?" His lips brushed against hers, teasing and tantalizing.

"That's a silly nickname."

Then his mouth was pressing on hers—warm, strong, and commanding. *It really does take your breath away,* she thought. Andrea felt like she was floating in time and space. She was numb except for the electrifying touch of his hand on her arm, his arm around her shoulder, and the rhythm of his kiss.

Finally, she pulled away shyly without looking at him.

"Wow," she said softly. He started to speak but she held her fingertips to his lips to stop him. "Home, Blackburn," she instructed.

He tousled her hair and started the motor. They drove slowly back the way they had come. The morning had given Andrea a giddy sense of liberation. The crisp, clean air, the bright sunshine now growing into the heat of the day, the natural joking and teasing they had fallen into— she couldn't remember when she had felt such abandon.

Abandon! That was obvious, she chided herself. Letting him kiss her like that. It was silly, of course. But how she had enjoyed it. She tasted her lips, remembering.

They were approaching the creek again. "Stop! I'll cross it my own way this time," she said, and started untying her shoelace.

"What?" he asked as he stopped the Jeep.

"It's not deep here. I want to wade across. I haven't done anything like that since I was a child," she said eagerly. Her shoes and socks in hand, she jumped gracefully out of the Jeep and made her way to the water. He followed.

She stepped from the warm sand onto the large stones in the water. Andrea gasped with the shock of the icy stream on warm, bare skin. She rapidly swished her feet around to warm them. "It's freezing! Why didn't you tell me?"

"Aw, it's not that bad." He laughed and scooped up

a handful of water and flung it on her. She ran from him squealing but when he was about to catch up with her she turned and kicked furiously, drenching him.

"Okay, okay. I give! Uncle!" He laughed, trying to shield himself from her barrage.

"Thank goodness," Andrea said breathlessly. "I think I've suffered permanent injury from these rocks on my bare feet."

She flopped down on a smooth grassy spot on the bank of the creek. His joyous, hearty laugh seemed to vibrate through her. *This is all too wonderfully, insanely perfect and illogical,* she thought.

"Let me see your foot." He knelt beside her and brushed the grass and sand off her sole. His work-roughened hands were warm, strong, and gentle. *I know his touch exactly now,* she thought. He bent over her, his face very near hers. Andrea was afraid to look up and meet his gaze. She was afraid to reveal how good it felt to have him near.

He examined her other foot and she had to shift her position. Did he push her back gently or did she pull him down? She couldn't tell. All she knew for certain was the weight of his embrace, the eager press of his mouth and the pounding of her heart. She timidly traced the line of his jaw with her fingertips. The touch set off sparks and he cradled her close to him. She ran her fingers through his wavy hair and responded hungrily to his searching kiss. He was still a stranger to her but it felt so natural, so right to be with him this way.

Her senses had never been more aware. Her hands slid down his arms and back. His shirt was damp and clung to his muscles. Wonder and warmth passed through Andrea like an electric current. Then his mouth broke away from hers.

He steeled himself and drew a long breath while he held her for another moment and stared at the faraway horizon. Andrea saw his jaw work as he clenched his teeth and set his mouth determinedly. There was a look of pain and anger in his eyes, then it was veiled by his customary controlled expression. He rolled away from her and stood.

"Guess we better get you home and dried off," he said regretfully. She nervously fumbled her shoes on and they silently returned to the old Jeep.

The jovial companionship was gone along with the intimacy. Andrea didn't want to question why. She didn't want to think she had been foolish. She just wanted to savor the feelings of the morning, without her customary practicality.

She had put the anger and suspicions of the previous day out of her mind until now. She didn't want them to return. She didn't want more complications in her life. She didn't want to think. She wanted to feel and enjoy, like she had all morning.

They passed close to a ridge that dropped into a valley. "That's lovely. Let's drive over that way," she suggested, breaking the silence.

"Not now," he said uneasily.

"Why not?" She tried to sound lighthearted again. "Isn't it on my . . . Mantilla Bluff property?"

"It is. Land's not much good down there. We try to keep the stock away from there so they won't break a leg or fall."

"Well, I'm not stock. I won't fall. Take me down there. The landscape is beautiful."

He looked at her as if he were trying to decide something. He decided. "I'll take you down there another time. Not now."

Andrea watched him in puzzlement. He was obviously agitated. Why? What could there be about the little valley that was so mysterious? Or did he just want to get away from her?

There was an unfamiliar car at the ranch house when they returned. Andrea looked questioningly at Blackburn, expecting him to recognize the vehicle. He did, judging from his uneasy glance at Andrea and the strained cheerfulness he put on.

"More neighbors come to call," he said.

They entered the house through the kitchen. Espy looked up from her cooking to chuckle at their appearance. *Blackburn always brings me in looking like a wreck,* Andrea thought.

A strikingly beautiful woman awaited them inside and surveyed their damp attire from the railing overlooking the dining room.

"My, I didn't know we'd had rain," she said archly.

Chapter Five

T he woman was indeed beautiful, with silky black hair that hung thick and straight to her shoulders. She pushed one side of it behind her ear and unbuttoned her suit jacket as she leaned a curvaceous hip against the railing. Andrea was amazed at how the gesture changed the woman's whole look from business to . . . well, the dress under the jacket was a clinging red knit. Andrea wished she could capture that sort of dazzling presence on stage.

"Rachel, what brings you here?" Blackburn asked uneasily, straightening his hair and clothing.

"Why, darling, I had to welcome our new neighbor," she answered, her voice low and purring. "As I see you've been doing." Her smile for Andrea was friendly but there was disdain in her dark eyes.

"Mrs. Keith is your neighbor to the north," Blackburn explained.

"Senator Rachel Carswell Keith and no Mrs., please. I got rid of the slime ages ago. You call me Rachel, dear."

Andrea didn't like her. The woman made her feel like she was an intruder in the other woman's domain and Andrea didn't like it. She didn't like hearing her call Blackburn "darling," and most of all, she didn't like admitting it.

"Rachel is our representative in the state legislature," Blackburn said.

"And as the local political bigwig I want you to know that I'll help you dispose of Mantilla Bluff as quickly as possible," Rachel said casually. "I'm sure you don't have the time or expertise and there are many ways I can . . . expedite things."

Andrea bristled at the woman's condescension. "That's very kind of you, but Mr. Blackburn and I have hardly had a chance to review matters." She couldn't believe she heard herself stalling the same business she'd been so eager to hurry along. "I'm sure I can manage everything without bothering you."

"I'm not easily bothered," Rachel answered, her gaze steady and ominous underneath her smile.

"Miss Zanovya wants to take a look at the place and I'll see that she understands all the legal entanglements and business considerations of the ranching operations, gas wells, and other things about the ranch," Blackburn said. He was interrupting Rachel but he was looking at Andrea hopefully.

He thinks I've taken his side and accepted his slow method of settling the estate, Andrea realized. *Well, I'm still keeping to my time schedule, but without Senator Keith's help.*

"So much fuss isn't necessary," Rachel said, slinking her way down the steps. "I know operations of this size can be unwieldy and certainly very slow to move in to-day's market. I'm sure Miss Zanovya wants to get back to her life in the East.

"Run along and clean up, dear," she ordered Andrea. Linking her arm with Blackburn's, she said, "Darling, Esperanza has cooked a mountain of food as usual, so we'll all stay for lunch. Will's with me and that dreadful Lawler woman called to say she'd be coming over later."

Andrea stomped up the stairs, throwing a hostile glare

at Rachel's companion coming in from the living room. *Imagine being dismissed from my own dining room in that patronizing tone of voice,* she thought with irritation. *So why am I doing exactly as she commanded?*

And why should I care what she calls him? Andrea scolded herself as she rifled through her closet. *Why do I feel so territorial about Blackburn? And it's not going to be be my dining room long, anyway. But what business is it of hers?*

She looked for something feminine to wear to compete with Rachel's simple but sensational dress. The best she could do was an emerald-green blouse that set off her eyes, a gold chain, and clean slacks. Not exactly a challenge to the predatory senator, she decided, then reminded herself she didn't care. *I was caught unexpectedly and I was just embarrassed to be seen looking so messy, that's all. I'm going back to New York as soon as possible, anyway.*

But she hurried to dry her hair and change.

When Andrea returned Rachel was regaling Blackburn and Will Campbell, introduced as her legislative aide, with details of a recent political gathering. Apparently she knew everyone of importance in the state. "So, of course, you know what Ann said to that—'Grandma's slow too, but she's old'—and the whole railroad commission gave in."

Will laughed heartily, then graciously seated Andrea next to him at the dining room table. He was nice looking, well dressed, and almost too well coifed, like a television newsman. Andrea wondered if he laughed that enthusiastically at all the senator's jokes. Blackburn wasn't paying much attention even though Rachel sat next to him, leaned in his direction, and touched his arm every few seconds. Espy finished loading the table with food and joined them.

Rachel kept up her monologue about locally important people and events, defying Espy's efforts to steer the talk to more general topics.

"Patterson tried to get me to join them on the junket but I told him I always return home to my constituents whenever possible," Rachel continued. She gave Blackburn a coy look.

Campbell smiled again at Andrea and asked, "How do you find our part of the country, Miss Zanovya?"

Before she could speak, Rachel turned to them. "I'm sure it's terribly dull and quiet compared to the cities she's used to. Isn't it, dear?"

Without waiting for a reply, she put a hand on Blackburn's shoulder and cooed, "Blackie, honey, we missed you at the Taylors' last night. Ellen and Brewster were at it again. Oh, the arguments and catty remarks."

She snaked a red-nailed hand up to smooth Blackburn's shirt collar. "Honestly, I don't know why those two stay married, do you? Unless they love as well as they fight."

Andrea stabbed savagely at her green beans.

"Mantilla Bluff is very quiet," she said brightly. "But I wouldn't say my trip has been dull." She smiled sweetly at Rachel and watched out of the corner of her eye for a reaction from Blackburn. There was none. He toyed with his food.

"Well, being chauffeured around by this old country boy here," Campbell said, grinning and nodding toward Blackburn, "can't be much fun, Miss Zanovya. I'm sure we could find something better to amuse you. Just consider me at your disposal."

"Please, Will, Miss Zanovya is just here to sign a few papers," Rachel interjected again. "She hasn't time to become the next victim of your inestimable charm. And I'm sure she has someone even more charming eagerly awaiting her return to New York or wherever.

"In fact, Miss Zanovya, the airline schedules in Amarillo are not convenient, so I'll be happy to send you home on my daddy's—er, the Carswell company plane. You can leave anytime you want to. See to that, Will dear."

She turned back to Blackburn and said something too low for the others to hear. Andrea looked on in furious silence. She glanced uncomfortably at Campbell. Apparently he was used to the senator's high-handedness, for he kept smiling and said, also in a low tone, "I hope you won't rush off too soon. We really do like to show off our western hospitality."

Andrea smiled back at him. "Speaking of western hospitality," she said, "I couldn't possibly think of leaving before the traditional Merrick barbecue. Especially since I'm the hostess this year."

That got a reaction from everyone.

"Mighty fine," Campbell said enthusiastically. "You be sure and save me the first dance."

Rachel struggled to hide her dismay, "Really, my dear, that is too generous of you." She tapped her long, manicured nails nervously on the table.

Espy, who had watched all this in amiable silence, smiled slyly and nodded.

But it was Blackburn's reaction that Andrea enjoyed most of all. His facial expression, for a brief moment only, was a contorted battle between incredulity and suspicion. Then he leaned back and casually relaxed his lanky frame in the chair. This attitude of lazy unconcern, Andrea had already learned, appeared when he was deepest in thought.

I've given you quite an interesting morning, haven't I, Mr. Blackburn? Andrea thought. She almost giggled in triumph.

Espy began to clear the dishes and Andrea rose to help her. Blackburn finally gave her a slight, curious glance as she passed his chair. She returned a wide-eyed, innocent smile. But she too was questioning why she had volunteered the barbecue and stuck herself here through the weekend.

As she was about to leave the kitchen, Espy said, "He don't care nothing about her."

"Excuse me?"

"She's been after him since they was kids. She hasn't got him yet." Espy gave her a knowing look.

"You mean Blackburn and Mrs. Keith? It's of no consequence to me." She was determined to make that statement become the truth. *He means nothing to me,* Andrea reminded herself, *so why should I care if that woman thinks she owns him?*

This morning would be a pleasant memory though. Andrea hadn't had a day in the country like that for years. She hadn't had a day of such carefree abandon. A dancer's life was filled with rehearsals, instruction, and performance. If she neglected the instrument of her body for more than a few days she risked injury or, equally worrisome, a poor performance.

Andrea didn't mind the routine nor the single-minded dedication dance asked of her. She couldn't remember not dancing. Dancing had been her parents' life and it had naturally become hers. She had talent and the beginnings of a brilliant career.

Already she was about to equal her mother's success. If she could dance "Giselle" this season, she would fulfill her dreams—her mother's dreams, really. Her mother had been gone for years, but Andrea felt that if she won this role, if she achieved this goal, she would finally win her mother's complete approval and love.

So why was she even considering staying in Texas? She wasn't. The morning had been very nice. Interesting, fun, and as for Blackburn—well, the man was certainly attractive, but she had Nigel. Nigel would never have grabbed her and tried to kiss her the first day they met or lie damp on the creek bank with her. She had felt more passion in Blackburn's brief embraces than she had ever felt with Nigel, but she couldn't really know what was behind Blackburn's advances. His behavior had been perplexing since she had first heard of her inheritance.

And Nigel understood her. Nigel shared her life in the dance. Nigel loved her and she loved him. So, soon, she would return to him. That was the only reasonable course of action.

She began as soon as she rejoined them in the dining room.

"Senator Keith, it was a pleasure to meet you, but I'm afraid you'll have to excuse me just now," she said. "I have a lot of business to take care of if I'm going to throw a party and still be able to leave on Sunday."

"I quite understand, Miss Zanovya," Rachel said smoothly. "However, this was not merely a social call on my part. I told you I would be happy to expedite your business here.

"So, out of consideration for dear old Mr. Merrick— and for you too, Miss Zanovya—I am prepared to make you a very reasonable offer for the whole ranch."

Andrea wasn't sure she understood. Perplexed and with a trembling hand, she took the sheaf of papers Rachel had drawn out of her bag. She glanced at them. She wasn't prepared for this.

"You want to buy Mantilla Bluff?" Andrea asked.

Blackburn exploded out of his chair. "For Pete's sake, Rachel! She hasn't even had a chance to see the house yet. You don't even know if she intends to sell."

"Calm down, darling." Rachel stepped close to him and stroked his back. "Of course, she intends to sell," she purred. "What on earth is there for her here?"

He paced the room in agitation. "Hold on, Rachel. I'm sure Miss Zanovya doesn't want to be rushed into anything."

"And I'm sure she has other matters more important to her than sitting around in our little town worrying about cows and crops."

Andrea couldn't speak. She wanted to sell the ranch, of course, but now this offer seemed too sudden. She felt the same turmoil Blackburn was exhibiting.

"Well, this is certainly something I must consider," she said, trying to regain control of the situation. She wanted to look as poised and confident as the other woman.

"Indeed, Miss Zanovya," Rachel agreed. "I've had Will draw up the necessary papers. These will simply release all property and pertinent rights to me for the sum noted here."

She thrust a second sheaf of papers into Andrea's hands. "I trust you'll find that adequate."

Adequate was was hardly the word. Andrea stifled a gasp when she saw the numbers.

Rachel went on quickly, "This is your copy of the agreement. Will can fax a copy to your own lawyer this afternoon. I'm sure you'll want advice from someone besides Blackie. He's a wonderful lawyer, of course, but you hardly know him, do you?"

Blackburn crossed to her. "Andrea, you haven't seen

the will or the rest of the ranch or the house. We haven't even talked about business yet.''

"No, we haven't, have we, Mr. Blackburn? When shall we?" Andrea asked pointedly.

"Blackie's just an old country boy, aren't you, honey?" Rachel said. "Takes his own sweet time to do everything."

"Oh, I wouldn't exactly say that," Andrea murmured.

Rachel glanced at her sharply but continued, "Now, you just say the word and we'll have these papers signed and you can be on your way in no time."

"You can't, Andrea," Blackburn pleaded. "You have a responsibility to Mantilla Bluff."

"Do I?"

"And to the old man!"

"Why?" she asked.

He stared at her, looking shocked and unbelieving.

"She has a responsibility to herself," Rachel said. "If she wants to sell—and what else can she do—you know she won't get a better offer. Not for a long, long time. Unless you can offer her something."

There was a long, tense silence. Blackburn looked down, defeated.

Rachel was prepared to take advantage of it. "Blackie, darling, I know how you felt about old Mr. Merrick. And I know how you care for Mantilla Bluff. But who better to buy it from her than me? I grew up out here too. I know what's best for this country and for Mantilla Bluff."

She sidled very close to him and spoke so low that Andrea wasn't sure she heard, "I made you an offer too. Remember?"

He stiffened and his jaw clenched.

"I'll look this over and give it serious consideration, Mrs. . . . er, Senator Keith," Andrea said.

Rachel turned and smiled her cold smile. "I'm sure you'll find it's the best you can do."

Andrea shrank from the woman's powerful self-assurance. She wanted to look to Blackburn for help but she didn't dare. Rachel would see her confusion and weakness.

"Well," Rachel said haughtily, "I suppose I must get back to the office. I hope we don't have another 'rain-storm' hit."

Blackburn grabbed his hat from the sideboard and slammed out of the house through the kitchen. Andrea saw an eager gleam of triumph in Rachel's eyes.

"I'll be in touch, Miss Zanovya." She swept out, Will following with a reluctant smile at Andrea.

Espy was ready to leave too, and a few minutes later Andrea stood enjoying the stillness of the house. What a day it had been, and it was just past noon. A little more than twenty-four hours ago she had been home in New York, busy planning her dancing life, willing to give a few days to this strange and intriguing prospect of inheritance. But certainly not envisioning anything like the events of the past day—Blackburn's mysterious behavior concerning the ranch, KittyLu's sweet and silly nature, Rachel's astounding offer.

And Blackburn's explosive kiss.

Each time she thought of Blackburn's touch she had an eerie, unbalanced feeling. Even with other people in the room, his presence quickened her pulse and clouded her concentration. He was so irritating and arrogant and —no, she amended the thought, he was sometimes frank and plainspoken, and that certainly made her feel uncomfortable.

Other times—the friendly, intimate times—he was an

enigma, open and giving in his physical actions but some-how remote and angry inside.

He had been quite alarmed when it appeared she would sell Mantilla Bluff to Rachel. Why? What could it matter to him? If he was involved with Rachel, why wouldn't he welcome the sale?

Why did he get so outraged when she mentioned Mr. Merrick? She walked into the living area as if she needed to get away from the lingering presence. She was gazing at the bookshelves with their mixed collection of books, newspapers, junk mail, and remnants of farm tools. Who was this old man?

Well, he had chosen her to settle his estate and part of that task was to clear out the house and get it ready for sale. It was time to get on with the odious task of sorting through Merrick's personal papers. Perhaps the answer to her questions could be found somewhere in this house.

Blackburn jerked the gears and pushed the aged Jeep's motor to its roaring speed limit. He had to get away from that house quickly, before he strangled one or both of those women. *Rachel and her tricks to get just what she wants,* he thought irritably.

Andrea and her cold-hearted disregard for the old man. How she could ask "why?" when he talked about re-sponsibility was beyond him. Just about the cruelest thing he had ever heard a woman say, and he'd heard plenty of cruel things from women.

He'd finagled to get her to come to Texas just like he promised Merrick, but she'd been indifferent to the ranch, interested only in how she could get rid of it. Then here came Rachel waving a high-dollar contract under her nose just when he thought he might have Andrea starting to get to know the place.

He knew Rachel was hot to have Mantilla Bluff. What he couldn't figure was exactly why. Her daddy had a spread nearly as nice and Rachel didn't like ranch life anyway. She'd rather be in Austin wheeling and dealing with the politicians or anywhere more populous than Dallam County, the center of attention. Now the vixen had been dogging his heels trying to get her hands on Merrick's holdings. Still, he hadn't expected her to sneak up on Andrea with an offer so soon.

His timing had been off from the beginning and now he felt like he was losing the slim control of the situation he might have had. He'd promised the old man he'd come through for him and it was important to keep that promise. After all, Blackburn had been lonely too. Not quite like Merrick, he would have to admit. But the pain was real and in those rare moments when he allowed himself to think about Helen he could see himself just like Merrick— living a good life, but alone.

Blackburn needed physical exertion to drive the agitation from his mind. He stopped in the pasture where two of the Gonzales boys were working their cattle. "Victor, Antonio, *¿como estas?*" he said, stepping out of the Jeep and pulling on leather work gloves. The two men jerked their chins in acknowledgement. He nodded a greeting. Shaking hands was a cultural trait not shared by the Hispanics. He wondered if Andrea knew that. *Oh, well,* he thought, *there's a lot she doesn't know and she may not be around long enough to learn.*

"Could you use a hand?" he asked as he watched one strong man struggle to hold and vaccinate a large calf.

"I could always use a hand when my brother is 'helping' me so much," Antonio said, grinning at the man who watched from atop his horse.

"He's just not *fuerte* enough to handle those calves by

himself,'' Victor teased. "He expects me to cut 'em out and doctor 'em both?''

Blackburn laughed at their good-natured squabbling. "Let me try out that roan. I saw you training him and he looked like he might make a good cutting horse.''

"Go ahead, my butt's tired anyway,'' Victor said.

Blackburn climbed astride the sleek animal and trotted him back and forth a few yards to get the feel of the reining that would be required. The horse was quick and responsive. He weaved into the herd and cut in between a calf and its mother. *It's lucky the cutting horse knows his job so well,* Blackburn thought, *for this cowboy's mind isn't on his work.*

He charged at the calf and the bleating animal tried to run around the horse toward its mother. Blackburn reined gently to the left; the horse pivoted on his rear legs and shuffled his front hooves, gracefully heading the skittish youngster toward the two men on the ground. The quarter horse was much quicker than the calf and soon ran it right where it needed to be.

This is just what I'm trying to do with Andrea, he thought. *Cut her out from the herd and drive her in the right direction. Trouble is, it's exactly opposite from the way she wants to go.*

He laughed aloud at the comparison and the image of how she would react if she knew about it. She would draw up in her haughty Ice Princess pose, frost him with a glare, and make some kind of snooty remark.

Or she might laugh and go him one better by comparing him to the horse. She certainly wasn't the Ice Princess this morning. Blackburn remembered the feeling of elation he had when he first saw her this morning jogging across the pasture.

He had wondered at the time why he was so glad to

see the woman who had so far been more trouble than she was worth. But she looked so happy and full of life loping gracefully into the prairie wind—and right fetching in her tight jeans and clinging top.

He could still imagine the feel of her body pressed against him, so soft, yet with an underlying feeling of strength. The sights and sensations of the morning flooded over him in a jumble. He saw her tangled mop of hair, her long, lithe legs, her smile as she leaned against the Jeep, her frown at the taste of wheat kernels, her gasp of shock when he splashed her.

Sharing the ranch with her had been the best time he'd had in a long time. He knew she understood the land now and the value of the what the land represented. It was great that she could pick up on all that without his having to explain it. He liked being able to communicate with her without words. Like when he teased her by holding the barbed-wire fence open for her this morning, he thought with another chuckle. The little imp had bested him on that one and when she looked up at him with such sass he knew he was in big trouble. He'd struggled all morning to keep his eyes and his hands to himself, but when she stood there so warm and close and tousled he wanted to devour her.

His natural suspicion of willing women stopped him then. And later, lying on the creek bank with her, he was able to stop only because the last few years of disciplined denial had made it hard for him to handle much more than one real, caring embrace. Any more of her eager response and he knew he'd turn back into the fool that had tried to make a decent human being out of Helen. And he wouldn't go through that again.

If there was ever to be a woman in his life again he wouldn't be the one to do all the giving.

* * *

She felt uneasy entering the old man's upstairs bed-room, as though she were intruding on a stranger—a deceased stranger. There was an old, worn leather easy chair beside a cluttered desk. She ran her fingers over the oak. It was worn smooth and glossy from decades of use. There was something friendly and comfortable about it that made it seem almost familiar.

An envelope in the corner pigeonhole caught her eye. It was crisp and new among a desk full of ragged papers. She pulled it out and read *For Andrea* written in an elaborate, old-fashioned script.

A knot in her stomach chilled her through. *Oh, I wish I hadn't come on this,* she thought as she stared at the envelope. *I don't want to read this.*

Finally, she put on her father's disciplined attitude and took out the pages and began to read:

My dear little Andy, I knew you would find this. Your mother was a snoop too. . . .

Chapter Six

*C*uriosity that could K.O. the kitty was one of her more endearing qualities, the letter continued. Andrea felt it an affront to be hearing about her mother from this stranger, but she had to read on.

Lorraina lived life with a probing enthusiasm and zest that was very unusual for a young lady back then when I knew her best. She wanted to grab every bit of excitement and reward she could out of every minute.

Don't get me wrong. She wasn't loose. It wasn't just pleasure she was after. She just wanted to be totally alive. She was a passionate risk-taker. Lorraina wanted life to be electrifying every single moment. When I first met her in the orchestra's rehearsal hall she was trying to get a sound out of each instrument in the room. I thought she was trying to decide which one to study, but she said no, she wanted to study them all. Be a whole orchestra herself.

I laughed at her and told her it was impossible. She was so angry she yelled at me for ten minutes. In Russian! And, by golly, that semester she learned to play three stringed instruments and the flute. Just to show me up! She was making good progress on the oboe when she finally gave in and said maybe she couldn't be the whole danged orchestra. She also told me she wasn't really Russian. She learned the language to see if it helped her ballet performance. What a woman!

Andrea put the papers down and brushed tears from her eyes. Had her mother actually been such a silly, impetuous girl? It was so sweet and sad to think of her that way. To Andrea she had always been a mature, solemn, disciplined dancer. It was that maturity and seriousness Andrea had spent her life trying to emulate.

She walked to the window and looked out for a moment. The pastoral scene of the creek and trees now was as foreign to her as the idea of her mother shouting at a stranger in Russian. She ached with loneliness for her mother. It had been so long since she'd heard her voice.

She picked up the letter again.

You probably never knew her that way. She became very strictly regimented in her work. I imagine that was the side you saw. Unwavering dedication to her goal of being a great dancer and a perfect mother.

That's what she chose. I helped destroy that wonderful feeling of omnipotence she had. And, by doing that, I destroyed the very magic I had fallen in love with. When she realized she couldn't do everything, but had to choose and find priorities, she did choose. Quickly and finally and totally.

She chose dance over all that was offered to her. Over music and all her other talents. Over me. But I thought that was right for her.

I chose not to interfere. I thought that was right for me.

But in these last years, I've decided it wasn't

*right. I'll keep my promise to her. I won't go to you.
I won't contact you in any way. But I have to tell
you now. It's not right that you don't know somehow.
Then you can choose for yourself what to do with
the information.*

Andy, my sweet little Andy, I am your father.

Andrea stared at the page. She read the last sentence
again and again as waves of rage and confusion swept
over her. She crumpled the pages into a ball and threw
them down. She stared coldly at the lump until tears
welled in her eyes again.

She fled to the white bedroom. Mantilla Bluff gleamed
brightly in the afternoon sunlight. She hated the huge
ugly thing. She hated the hot tears streaming silently
down her cheeks. She hated Merrick. She hated—

Blackburn's Jeep roared around the bluff and parked
beside the terrace. He jumped out and sauntered up to
the house, whistling jauntily.

Andrea struggled for control. She washed her tear-
streaked face, marched back to the other room, and
grabbed the crumpled papers. She smoothed them quickly
and ran down the stairs to the kitchen.

Blackburn was there leaning against the refrigerator
holding a half-empty glass of milk. It irritated her the
way these people always treated this house as their own.

Blackburn wiped the milk off his lip and said, "I'm
glad you decided—"

"Did you know about this?" she demanded harshly,
rattling the papers at him.

"What is it?"

"It's a letter to me from . . . him." Her voice wavered
with emotion. "I found it on his desk upstairs. Did you
know it was there?"

He carefully put down the glass and took a step toward her. She flinched away from him.

"No, I didn't know how he was going to—"

"How he was going to deal with me?" she interrupted. "Do you know what he said in here?"

"I was privileged to be Dolf's good friend." His voice was now hard and defiant.

"So you knew. You knew all this time and didn't say a word to me about it," Andrea accused. She glared at him, all her anger at the unknown man focused on his "good friend."

"Why didn't you tell me? Warn me? Prepare me somehow?"

Blackburn edged close to her, but seemed to change his mind about touching her.

"He wanted you to come here and see the place. Maybe you'd remember and maybe you'd want to have some connection to him after all. He thought it might change your mind about him," he said, his voice catching. "He loved this place and he wanted you to love it too."

Andrea stood clutching the papers and not looking at Blackburn. He gently took the papers from her hand. "This is private between you and him, but . . . what did he say to upset you so much?"

"What did he say? He said . . . he claims he's my father! It's a lie, of course. I can't believe he would malign my mother and then expect me to acquiesce by accepting a legacy from him!"

"Claims?" He frowned and his expression was thunderous again. "Malign your mother? Just what do you mean?"

"Malign: to disparage, put down, say bad things about. You've been to college. It's a common enough word," she said bitterly.

He glowered at her, his eyes darkening. "Dolf Merrick wasn't good enough to be your father? You snooty—"

"No, no, that's not what I mean." Andrea shook her head impatiently. "I mean how could he be my father? I know my mother would never be unfaithful to my fath —her husband."

"Oh, I see. That explains a lot." Blackburn paced the room, thinking. "We thought your mother had told you. She told him she would eventually. But he hadn't heard from her in years."

"What? You knew about this? You thought . . . " Andrea stopped, confused as well as angry. "It can't be true. I would have known or sensed something or . . . " Her defiant stance wilted. She turned away from his sympathetic gaze.

All these people had acted as if she had some relationship with Merrick, she thought. They had expected her to grieve over his death. And she knew there had to be some reason for this inheritance. It did make a crazy kind of sense.

"KittyLu said her mother knew mine. Oh, no, who else knows about this?"

She buried her face in her hands. Humiliation flooded over the outrage. "This inheritance mystery started out as just a curiosity, a tantalizing sort of nuisance," she said, her voice shaky. "I was touched by an old man's eccentric generosity. And if I couldn't help find a rightful heir, then I . . . I would accept the windfall."

She retreated to the corner of the room, away from Blackburn's looming presence, and spoke as if talking only to herself. "Now I find him claiming that I truly am the rightful heir, his daughter. Everyone around here knows about it and probably believes it, when it can't be. It's ridiculous. Preposterous!"

Andrea felt hot tears welling up again. She drew a long, deep breath and bit her lip to regain her composure. She wouldn't let Blackburn see her crumble.

"Well?" he asked calmly from behind her. "What are you going to do about it? I mean, besides pitch a fit at me?"

Startled, she turned and looked at him.

"I don't know."

She thought of calling Nigel, but she knew what he would say. He'd tell her to quit being so emotional about the past, as if it didn't matter.

"I don't know." she repeated softly. Blackburn came to her. He folded his huge, strong arms over her, bringing her against his chest and closing her off from the world. He stroked her hair while she wept.

After a time, Blackburn said, "The old man was awful lonely for you."

He sniffed and cleared his throat. "He thought you knew but didn't care."

Andrea cried harder.

"He made me promise to bring you to Mantilla Bluff. To see if there was any of him in you. This place, this land was so much a part of him."

Andrea pictured the old man who had spent his years building this ranch, living in this house, thinking of her.

She finally lifted her head enough to look at Blackburn's chest. She wiped at his wet shirt. He handed her a handkerchief.

"No charge," he said.

She looked up into his face. His deep brown eyes were gentle and understanding.

"Don't be so nice to me. I can't stand it when you're nice to me," she said through her sniffles.

His laughter filled the kitchen. "Okay." He gave her

a friendly squeeze, released her, and reached for his glass of milk. "Now about selling the place to Rachel—"

"Oh, Blackburn, I can't think about that right now. Get out of here and leave me alone for a while. Just go away! I can't think at all when you're around."

"Mmm, I'm glad to hear it." He swept her into his arms and kissed her hard and long. She forgot everything but the feel of his embrace. He crushed her to him with a new eagerness and joy. His hands stroked her back.

She gasped for air. "Mr. Blackburn!"

"Let me stay and keep you from thinking," he whispered into her hair.

"Go!"

"I'll be close by, if you change your mind."

He pressed her to him in another consuming crush. Then he was out the door. She wanted him back. She rushed to the door, but stopped and watched him drive away. *You're crazy*, she told herself. *But I don't know if you're crazy for wanting him to stay or for letting him go.*

Andrea hung up the telephone again and leaned back on the bed. She was tired and frustrated. That was the sixth call and none of her parents' old friends had any new information for her. She still couldn't believe it. The idea that her mother had been unfaithful to her father was ludicrous. Oh, she wasn't naive. She knew things happened between people. But her parents were such sensible people. And how could Merrick, an old Texas cowboy, have met her mother at the conservatory?

Her parents' marriage wasn't perfect. She knew that, of course. Her mother was a great dancer who spent most of her time working. It took great dedication and grueling hours of practice to achieve what she had. That sort of life left little energy for husband and child. Lorraina Powell Zanovya was a greater success than Andrea's father—the man she knew as her father.

He was a dancer too. Competent and always in demand, but not the star that Lorraina was. At that period of time and even in the creative professions, such an imbalance was a strain on any marriage.

They had worked on their relationship with the same solemn concentration they worked on everything else, and it had held together, not joyously but pleasantly enough. They approached parenthood in the same manner. Andrea had the necessary affection and attention to make her a proper young lady. She had always wanted more, so she threw herself into ballet hoping to earn their love and esteem by excelling in it.

After phoning several of their old friends, Andrea realized even more how little she really knew the people who should have been closest to her.

She leaned forward and rubbed her eyes with the heels of her hands. *Who else?* she asked herself. *Who else is there to ask? I must know for sure.*

She picked up her address book and looked through it again, this time carefully trying to read even the old names she had marked through. Miss Thornby, her mother's teacher and friend from long ago. She'd know. *If she's still alive,* Andrea thought.

She dialed the number and was so grateful to hear the old lady's sprightly voice answer.

"Hello, Miss Thornby! It's Andrea Zanovya. How are you?" she began. The voice she heard in reply was just the same as ever.

"Well, I'm too old and stiff to lift my foot to the barre and too cranky to tell others how, so I'm virtually useless," the cheerful, raspy voice said. "But it's good to hear from you. It's been so long."

"Yes, much too long."

"What's new with you, dear?"

"Well, actually, I was curious about something." Andrea tried to keep her voice light and casual. "I thought you might be able to tell me about it."

"Certainly, Andrea, but it must be something big for you to come to me after so long," Miss Thornby said with the frankness that Andrea remembered was characteristic of her old teacher.

"Oh, I was just wondering how my mother and father met." She tried to sound casual. "I don't think I ever heard the story."

"Let me see. I guess it was when they were in Hartford. Um, Lorraina went from the National Ballet of Canada to Hartford, and when she came back to Pittsburgh after that, she had Andres with her. Yes. that was it," she said. "We were all a little surprised. But they were both terrifically interested in some new choreographer. Can't remember who that was now, but they were sure he was going to be the next Balanchine. I think that's what drew them together.

"Anyway, they made a good team. Always danced together."

"I suppose they were thrilled when I came along? Or was my arrival untimely?" Andrea tried to sound as though she were joking.

"Oh, you were the pet of the whole company. You know that!"

"Yes, but what I need to know is . . . were they really happy to have me? Were they happy together at the time?" She couldn't keep the urgency out of her voice.

There was a long pause at the other end of the line.

"Let's get down to brass tacks, Andrea," Miss Thornby said sternly. "What is it you're after?"

"Was Andres my father or was it a man named Merrick?"

"I thought it was something besides a trip down memory lane that made you call me," said the old woman. "Lorraina had you right after she left the conservatory. A year before she married Andres. I'm surprised you haven't figured that out before now."

"And Merrick? Who was he?" Andrea choked on the words.

"Well, my dear, I knew your mother when she was a student at the conservatory," Miss Thornby said. "And when I worked with her at Pittsburgh the first time she danced there, she was different. Much more serious. She was devoted to you, of course, but as far as I know she never told anyone about what went on with your father."

"Then you don't know Merrick?"

"Yes, I do," she continued. "He was a music instructor at the conservatory. Quite an interesting, complex man, actually. Much older than your mother. My stars, nearly as old as I was.

"They were quite an item, as we used to say. You don't know what a tempestuous girl your mother was, Andrea. I never knew what happened between them, but I guess you've figured it out. Is it so important? Now?"

"I really don't know, Miss Thornby," Andrea said at last. She was even more tired and bewildered than before this confirmation.

"You are who you are, who you always have been. Aren't you?" the old woman snapped.

"Oh, certainly . . . I guess." Was that it? Did it make a difference to her identity? Her ability?

"How did you come across Merrick?" Miss Thornby asked.

"I didn't really," Andrea answered with difficulty. "He . . . he died recently and left his property to me. I'm . . . calling from his Texas ranch. I couldn't imagine why he made me his heir but people around here seemed to remember Mother. And know about me."

"So that's where they disappeared to," the old woman murmured. "And Lorraina never said anything about all this?"

Andrea fought to speak over the lump in her throat. "He wrote me a letter. I found it today. I just can't believe he was my father."

Her voice trailed off weakly. "I just don't understand."

"My child," the voice on the telephone said gently but matter-of-factly, "in my aged wisdom I can tell you that it's better to find out the truth and learn to live with it."

"Yes, well"—Andrea choked back tired tears—"I guess the truth is finding me whether I like it or not."

She thanked her elderly friend and assured her that she could handle the situation, remaining totally unconvinced herself. She put the telephone down wearily. The house was silent, but it didn't feel quite so empty to Andrea anymore.

She walked into the small storage room behind the stairs. Espy and her daughters had left everything in perfect order. Cardboard cartons were stacked neatly along the wall, each with a name scribbled in large letters on it. The one marked "Dwight" held strips of new leather, some small hand tools, and two finished leather belts. "Miss Amy" got a heavy box of classical records and sheet music. Andrea closed them up and left. It was too sad to see the remnants of a man's life being packed to give away.

She passed the living area, tidy and polished and ready for a new owner. She looked at Merrick's book collection. Many were fine leather-bound classics. "I guess you go to the local library," she told them.

She tried to picture the house with Rachel as owner. Would she live in it? Andrea couldn't imagine it not being lived in. It was a warm, comfortable, inviting home. It should be filled with people. What a shame, as KittyLu would say.

Andrea ached with tension and fatigue. She couldn't think about this any longer. All she wanted was to lie down and forget about this long, incredible day. She went upstairs and curled up on her bed. The crisp smoothness of the white pillow was cool against her cheek.

She saw the legal papers Rachel had handed her that morning. *This changes that,* Andrea thought. *I can't sell Mantilla Bluff to her, now. I'm no longer a disinterested outsider.*

But what am I?

She pondered that facedown on the bed for a while. Then she decided.

Determined is what I am, she thought, pushing herself off the bed and wiping her eyes. She scrubbed her face and inwardly grumbled at her mother for keeping secrets, that is, if Miss Thornby remembered correctly.

She brushed her hair vigorously and fastened it at the nape of her neck. The nerve of this stranger, she thought, claiming to be her father only after he was gone and couldn't be confronted. Well, she would find out as much as possible about Adolf Merrick and she would start with Mantilla Bluff.

The odious task of clearing the house for sale now

became an act of vengeance for Andrea. She would go
through all Merrick's papers and belongings and find
absolute proof he was her father and why she never knew
it. Or, still likely, she believed, evidence that he was a
lonely old man who had imagined relationships that never
existed.

She returned to work at the desk in his bedroom and
soon had a stack of receipts and business papers she didn't
understand and an even larger stack of old junk mail. As
she examined every scrap of paper Andrea remembered
bits of long-ago conversations and childish questions
never fully answered. Her parents seldom spoke of family, hometowns, and school days. Andrea knew only the
basic, uninteresting facts about their pasts and about her
own childhood. It never seemed very important. *I never
seemed very important,* she thought.

No, that's absurd, she corrected herself. *They were
dedicated artists and they loved me very much. Children
are just selfish when it comes to their parents' time and
attention.*

Andrea shivered in the ghostly gloom of the silent
room. Then she heard a car approaching the house and
frowned in exasperation at the idea of another of Merrick's neighbors dropping in. She decided to get rid of
whoever it was before they got in the door.

Outside the sun was brilliant and the air was warm. A
huge white vintage Cadillac convertible rolled into the
yard and fluffs of teased platinum hair bobbed in the
driver's seat. Only KittyLu would drive a dinosaur like
that, Andrea thought with a smile.

"Hey-ey," KittyLu caroled as she bounced out of the
car. "So we're havin' a party! Right here at Mantilla
Bluff. I was so tickled when I heard. They're bringing

the beef over. Now, it's a little late but I think it'll make
just fine.''

Her heels clicked up the walk as she came to give
Andrea a squeeze and a peck on the cheek. Her dress,
scarf, matching belt, shoes, and handbags were lemon
yellow today. She always clicked, Andrea noticed—
bracelets, shoes, perky voice, and quick, bouncy little
movements.

KittyLu, as usual, was still talking. "Folks'll be bring-
in' things over for the party all afternoon, but that doesn't
mean we can't go shopping. I'll show you the big town
of Perico and we can boost the local economy. Don't you
think some pink or orange flowers could go in with the
red and yellow?''

Andrea hesitated, trying to decide which topic to address first. "I don't have time to go anywhere. I really
have to get something straightened out.''

"Plenty of time for that," KittyLu said. "Now, do
you have anything to wear to the barbecue? I know you
didn't foresee a party when you packed and you know
you will be the belle of the ball.''

Andrea thought of her impulsive decision to host the
barbecue and laughed wearily at herself. "Serves me right
for making rash invitations. Let me get my things.''

"Good girl!" KittyLu giggled.

A few minutes later they were flying down the dusty
road in the most enormous, luxurious car Andrea had
ever seen while KittyLu chattered about her husband's
office, her daughters' dance classes in Amarillo, and what
she might wear to tomorrow night's barbecue. Andrea
realized the only way to get into the conversation was to
interrupt.

"You say your mother knew my mother?" she asked.
"I had assumed Mr. Merrick was once a fan of my par-

ents, but I don't think they ever mentioned having been at Mantilla Bluff.''

KittyLu looked at her with wide eyes. ''Mama said your mama and you were last here when you were just a tiny thing. Y'all were here quite a spell. I reckon you were just too little to remember. Your mama never talked to you about it?''

Andrea shook her head. ''I knew nothing of Mr. Merrick until a few weeks ago when Mr. Blackburn contacted me about the inheritance. Since then I've been puzzled about the whole affair.''

KittyLu for once was speechless. She frowned and blinked in confusion.

Andrea continued, ''To tell you the truth, KittyLu, I'm embarrassed to be the legatee of a complete stranger.''

Once again KittyLu looked at her quizzically. ''But old Dolf . . . uh, I mean . . . Blackie said . . . well, he hopes . . . um, everybody in Perico would just love it if you took up residence at Mantilla Bluff! Our own famous star!''

Andrea smiled weakly, wondering if KittyLu knew of Merrick's claim, wondering why Blackburn wanted her to stay, wondering why anyone thought she might. Her life was elsewhere.

Finally the highway blended into the main street of a dusty, treeless town. A turn-of-the-century bank and a 1950's-style drugstore anchored opposite corners of the main intersection. KittyLu parked the car and they walked past the Texas Hotel, Nona's Café, the U.S. Soil Conservation office, and the Too Blond Salon before exploring Perico's shopping district.

KittyLu spoke to everyone they met, introducing Andrea and explaining that the barbecue was rescheduled to Mantilla Bluff. Everybody was friendly and wanted to know how her trip had been, what she thought of the ranch and the town, and when she could be expected at church or club meetings. By the time they had traveled two blocks Andrea was getting used to people's frank and undisguised interest in her. KittyLu was so eager for her to enjoy herself that she made several purchases just to please the woman. She also bought two Mexican dresses for herself and a turquoise ring for Nigel.

"I think I'll go ahead and get these little clown dolls for the twins," she told KittyLu at the small department store. "I think that will please Espy more than the gift I got for her."

"It will, it really will. Marcy and Espy are so crazy about those grandkids. They're so cute. You'll get to see them at the barbecue. Oh, and that white dress you bought today would be perfect to wear."

"By the way, KittyLu, I could use a good real estate broker to advise me on the ranch. Can you recommend one?"

"Sure can, honey. Me."

Andrea glanced at her in surprise and dropped the coins the clerk had just given her.

KittyLu giggled at her reaction. "Oh, I know you think I'm just a silly ol' dimwit without the sense God gave a goose. But I'm a durn good businesswoman."

Andrea took her packages and followed KittyLu out of the store. It was possible the woman's homespun silliness hid an incisive mind and, although she normally would have been much more cautious, Andrea wanted to trust her instincts now. Besides that, KittyLu's honest warmth elicited confidence. Andrea told her about Rachel's interest in the ranch.

"Of course, we all would love it if you'd keep Mantilla

Bluff,'' KittyLu said, looking at her hopefully. ''But if you're sure you want to sell. . . . ''

''I'm sure.''

''Well, I guess I shouldn't be so sad. We can ask a fortune and I'll make a huge commission. The consortium or Rachel, either one, can certainly afford it, so I guess everyone will be happy, but it seems a shame anyhow.'' She started the car and pulled away from the curb.

''What consortium? Who are they?'' Andrea asked.

''There's been some interest in the place by an industrial consortium from California. Merrick told my Henry a few months ago. It's all very hush-hush, although they did check into a few other places while they were here,'' KittyLu said, relishing the gossip. ''And I'll bet Miss Nosy Rachel knows all about it. That's what I figured the minute you told me what she was willing to fork over for the place. Without even having to dicker with you.

''I'll bet dollars to doughnuts that there's more to this than meets the eye, if you know what I mean.'' She paused long enough to give Andrea a knowing look.

Chapter Seven

Andrea didn't know what she meant. "Something's going on? Like what? It's a profitable business, apparently. Why would she have to be interested in anything but a good working ranch? The gas wells, is that it?"

"Why do you think Rachel is so interested in it?" KittyLu asked. "Her daddy's place is plenty big enough as it is. Why do you think she wants your place?"

Andrea had a sudden unexplained feeling of jealousy and possessiveness about the ranch.

KittyLu went on with a malicious giggle, "You don't think they're trying to surround Blackie and capture him that way for Rachel! She's been panting after Blackie since we were all in grade school."

"Yes, well, she's certainly beautiful and accomplished," Andrea said. She tried to sound neutral but KittyLu eyed her suspiciously.

Patting her cotton-candy hairdo, KittyLu said, "Humph. Too hard and sleek for my tastes. She needs softer edges—ruffles or something. Some of the milk of human kindness wouldn't hurt none either."

"She and Blackburn seem to be close friends." Andrea said coolly.

"Close?" KittyLu appeared to sense gossip. "What makes you say that?"

"Oh, nothing. He just seems to like her, that's all. And he acted as though there were some kind of . . .

92

relationship or history between the two or something,''
Andrea said.

"How?''

"Just something about their . . . uh, physical friendliness, and she said something about making him an offer.''
Andrea was afraid she'd revealed too much.

KittyLu fidgeted in her seat. "That scheming witch!
And that idiot! If he's giving in to her after all this time
I'll skin him alive! Blackie can't be that stupid. I know
he's been alone a long time, but he can find a hundred
women between here and the county line better than
that.'' KittyLu fumed. "Men are so ignorant when it
comes to pickin' the right partner.''

"It's hard to understand how any person makes the
choice,'' Andrea said, thinking of her mother.

"No, a woman knows her marriage is going to change
her life a lot more than it does a man's. Now I know
times are changing but they haven't changed that much
yet,'' KittyLu said, warming to her subject. "It's usually
the man's way of life that the woman adopts. You know
how it goes.''

"I think you're right, KittyLu. If a man and a woman
can't agree on things like where to live and how to co-
ordinate careers, for instance, I can see how that would
end a relationship,'' Andrea replied. "Even if there is a
very strong reason for staying together.''

"My, aren't we getting philosophical!'' KittyLu giggled. "Now here's where my Henry would say 'Watch
out before you tread on someone's toes and lose me a
client.' I'm always tellin' people what they oughta do.

"But you take Blackie and Rachel for an example.
She'd always be after him to live in Austin and later
probably Washington—I don't doubt that she's got that

kind of ambition—where she could hobnob with the fat cats all the time. And he'd want to stay here.

"Why, he hated that life when he had it. But she laps it up like a kitten in cream."

Andrea shook her head in confusion. "When Blackburn had that kind of life? What do you mean?"

KittyLu pulled up at a door on the side of the old bank building. It was stenciled "Lawler and Blackburn, Attorneys."

"Honey, there's lots of stuff I could tell you about your Mr. Blackburn," she said, "and I will someday. But I gotta go get my babies before my mother-in-law has 'em bad-mouthing me right along with her. Blackie said I could drop you off here and he'd take you home."

"Oh, well, I...uh," Andrea stammered as she climbed out of the car. She really wished she had gotten a better rental car yesterday. She hated depending on others for transportation, especially Blackburn.

"What about the sale contract?" she asked as KittyLu shifted her packages to Blackburn's old truck parked beside the curb. "When can you look it over?"

KittyLu shrugged and waved. "Anytime. Talk to you later!"

Andrea waved and watched her go. *What a dear scatterbrain,* she thought. *Sweet and funny and conniving— leaving me stranded here, relying on Blackburn again. As if I don't have enough on my mind without having to deal with some cowboy who always wants to...* She pushed the thought from her mind, turned resolutely, and entered the law office with determination.

It was paneled in dark, ancient walnut. Probably original woodwork of the Old West, she guessed. But the reception room was brightened by tasteful gray and green modern office furniture that matched a profusion of green plants and luxurious gray-green carpeting. The color of money, Andrea thought sardonically.

A perky young redhead looked up from her typing. "Miss Zinova?" she mispronounced. "Go right on in. He's expectin' ya."

Andrea took a deep breath and pushed on an old-fashioned carved door. The old wood paneling was polished to a dark glow. Equally ancient oak lawyer's bookcases lined two walls and modern decorator blinds covered another, leaving the room in late-afternoon gloom. At the far end of the room Blackburn lounged in a heavy leather chair, his long lanky legs stretched easily across a corner of the massive desk and the toe of one boot tapping lightly against it.

Andrea paused to watch him a moment before entering. He stared unseeing at the papers spread on the desk, his brow furrowed and his expression matching the foreboding gloom of the setting. She noted his rumpled shirt and the faded areas on his jeans where he had rubbed his hands often enough to soften the fabric. He raked his fingers through the hair falling onto his forehead. He had a way of looking threatening and charming at the same time, Andrea thought.

Blackburn saw her striding purposefully toward him, head regally erect and a strength in her manner. *I always thought dancers were supposed to be such delicate, graceful little butterflies or birds or willows or something,* he mused as he watched the sway of her body. Graceful, yes, he thought as his eyes took in her long shapely legs in the silky slacks. But this little butterfly had the strength of iron—a willow made of steel.

Looks like she's in the mood for another showdown, he noted as he met her steady gaze. *She's going to demand to know what she has to do so she can get the heck out of Texas. And this phone message might make a difference. He made a mental list of his options. I've shown her the property and she's completing the household inventory. She's discovered who her father was for the first time and claims it doesn't matter to her. How can it not matter? Sure, I can understand the shock, the denial at first. But she can't just ignore it. How cold can the woman be? How can a woman whose life is in the arts be so unemotional?*

She's not, he reminded himself. *I've seen her full of fire. I've felt the passion she has in her. I don't get it— fire and ice, all in the same woman. And I never know which is coming next.*

Thinking about her makes me edgy, he thought ruefully. He slowly drew his boots off the desk and eased out of his chair. He motioned toward the client's chair. "Afternoon," he said.

She remained standing. She looked sophisticated and chic even in casual clothes, he thought. But soft and feminine too. She really was something to look at. And to touch too, he added as a memory flashed through his senses. The memory was sharp and stinging in the strong emotion it stirred in him. He wanted to feel the hungry need she created in him. He wanted to feed it too. But instead he fought it and feared it.

He stepped around the corner of the heavy mahogany desk. She frowned, crossed her arms over her chest and sidled away from him. Was she afraid of all men, he wondered, or just him?

"Mr. Blackburn, I want to have a very frank talk with you," she began.

She wanted him to act like a lawyer now, so indeed he would. "Yes, ma'am, I know you want to see all the paperwork dealing with your inheritance and it's all here for perusal at your convenience.''

He picked up a thick stack of file folders from the desk and held them out to her. ''There are letters of administration showing that the court recognizes me as the administrator of the will,'' he said briskly. ''Probate has begun, but other possible heirs have up to one year to file protests for the legacy.''

She frowned and looked at the folders fearfully, then wrested them from him. He settled back into his leather chair. *What kind of stall could work this time?* he wondered. Probate and disposition really could be handled from New York or Boston. She could sell the ranch through an agent and never have to set foot on Texas soil again.

I could stall with alternate valuation, he thought. Just listing and assessing the current market value of every item could go on for months. But she could lease the place to Rachel or anyone else in the meantime. That wouldn't help much, he worried. *I need some time, just a little time.*

He thought of the long hours he'd spent listening to the old man reminiscing and the room seemed colder. He cleared his throat and continued brusquely, ''I have paid what outstanding debts there were, of course. There weren't many. He liked to live simply and straightforwardly.''

Andrea flinched and dropped the folders on the desk. She stared down at them, a grim expression on her face.

''Sorry,'' Blackburn said softly. ''I guess you don't see it that way. But he thought you knew about him and didn't . . . that your mother made you . . . ''

He was blowing it, he knew. He was supposed to make her want to stay, not rub salt in the wound and chase her off. He tried to go on. "Uh, the wells continue to operate as per agreement with Tenex Gas Company. As I said, all the papers are in there. You'll need to read over everything carefully."

Andrea paced impatiently. "Mr. Blackburn, I don't want to discuss all this. I mean, I do, of course, but . . . ." She stopped, her back to him. He could see she was finding it difficult to talk to him. He felt a thumping ache in his chest. She was wound tighter than a new rope and he wanted to see her laughing and carefree again. He needed to touch her and feel her melt into him again. He propped one boot on the edge of the desk and willed himself to quit thinking about her supple shape.

"I want to know what is going on here?" she demanded, turning suddenly.

His foot slipped to the floor with a jerk. He had forgotten what they were talking about. "Beg pardon?" he asked.

"What's going on at Mantilla Bluff that I don't know about?" she repeated.

What had KittyLu let slip? he wondered. His mind raced while he struggled to listen casually and keep his expression blank.

She was staring directly at him now. "There's some sort of consortium from California interested in the land and Senator Rachel Carswell Keith has offered me an exorbitant amount of money for the place," she said, strolling slowly and confidently forward.

"Consortium? Who are they?" His voice was leaden.

She looked like she was beginning to enjoy this. "Really, Mr. Blackburn, I don't think that's any of your business. Shall we proceed?"

"Yes, ma'am. Do you know how much the place is worth? Including oil and gas rights? Federal grazing leases? Stock on hand, equipment, water rights?'' he asked casually.

She blinked and shifted her weight. *Gotcha,* he thought. *She doesn't know anything about these things and she knows I know it. And she hates that I know it.*

''I can have appraisals done,'' she said at last.

''How do your buyers feel about the grass leases? Are they willing to wait until November to take possession of the pastureland or are they going to buy out the remainder of the leases?'' he asked.

''I . . . I haven't discussed the particulars with them yet. I told you it was just an offer. Two offers,'' Andrea snapped.

''Well, I wish you'd remember that the Gonzaleses are going to have to move all their cattle somewhere if they lose the subleases. You might be creating a problem for them,'' he said, looking at her calmly. ''Sure, you have a right to take the first offer that comes along. Or the biggest offer.''

''Well, I'm sure these are reasonable people. I would think that things of this nature can be handled amicably.'' Then she added acidly, ''If I decide to sell to Senator Keith perhaps you can prevail upon her to do things your way. She always seems eager to accomodate you.''

Women could be so petty, he thought in exasperation. ''Where did this attitude about Rachel come from?'' he asked. ''What has she ever done to you?''

''Nothing. Nothing at all,'' Andrea said, backing away and putting distance between them. ''In fact, her dropping in for lunch did me a great favor. She is willing to help me settle this affair and get on with my life, but all I've gotten from you is obfuscation, detours, and excuses.'' She stepped toward the door.

Blackburn decided he'd taken enough feminine

punches for one day. He leaped up to stop her. He grabbed her arm roughly and brought her around to face him. "What, exactly, is your problem, lady?"

"Blackburn, I simply want to get this over with."

"I don't get you. First you're all tensed up and rude to everyone, then you seem to relax and start taking an interest in the ranch," he said, searching her face for understanding. "Now you're in a rush to get out of here again, giving me the frost treatment when just a little while ago you were crying in my arms, so sweet and—"

She shook her head and pulled to free herself. "Let go of me. You're hurting my arm."

He unclenched his hands and let the breath ease out of him along with his anger. Andrea indignantly slipped out of his grasp and took a step back. He looked hard at her, trying to sort out the roil of emotions he was drowning in. For years he'd refused to let any woman rile him or get too close and in twenty-four short hours this one had him spinning in confusion like a pony on locoweed.

It hurt to breathe without shaking in rage, but he managed to speak gently. "It's really not smart to sell so quickly without studying all aspects of the deal. Particularly to outsiders. The old man wouldn't want it this way."

"I don't care!" she shouted. "I don't care! It's too late. It's too late to care what he wanted. It's what *I* want that matters now!"

"Unfortunately, it always mattered," he said bitterly.

She frowned questioningly. He turned and went back tiredly to his chair.

She continued, "And what I want is for you to do your job."

"My job is to look after you," he said, looking across

the room at her and wishing he hadn't promised the old man.

She met his gaze steadily. ''Your job is to take orders.''

He felt a surprising wave of admiration for her determination. He knew it wasn't her way, but she could be tough if she needed to be.

''Yes, ma'am.'' Without blinking he picked up a pad and pencil and felt a trace of a smirk tickle at the corner of his mouth.

Her nervousness was gone, replaced by that cold rage he'd seen once before. She marched across the space separating them, leaned over, and planted her hands on the desktop. ''I want to know what else there is that you haven't told me about this inheritance and I want to know why you haven't told me. And I want to know what else there is at the ranch that you haven't shown me. Like that valley I wanted to see this morning.''

He was so relieved he almost laughed out loud, but he kept his facial muscles stilled. ''I don't know what you're talking about, Miss Zanovya,'' he said evenly.

''Yes, you do know what I'm talking about, Mr. Blackburn. And you will tell me.''

Her hazel eyes bored into him. She was daring him to lie about it. And she was ready for him.

All right, he thought, *we've been playing power games since we met. Let's just see who has the power.*

He didn't move or look away, but smiled slowly. ''Some California consortium is interested in the property? Your broker tell you that?'' he asked. ''Well, there's always rich doctors and the like looking for tax shelters. Unfortunately, Mantilla Bluff manages to turn just enough profit each year to be a bad investment for such hogs feeding at the public trough.''

Andrea glared suspiciously at him while she drew herself erect and folded her arms impatiently. He thought he heard the soft tapping of her foot on the plush carpet. "And the honorable member of the legislature?" she asked, her voice rising angrily. "Is she willing to spend a small fortune just on a tax shelter?"

"Ah, Rachel's always got her own agenda," he said casually. He wondered why Andrea clenched her fists and bit her lip.

She went on with obvious difficulty. "And I suppose you're going to assure me with all your country charm that there's nothing you haven't told me about the ranch? I can hardly wait to hear you tell me not to worry my pretty little head."

"You want me to show you the east valley pasture? Come on, I'll take you there right now. We kept the last of Merrick's herd down there."

He rose immediately, grabbed his hat, and opened the door for her. She looked at him uncertainly, then scooped the files he had offered her into her arms and went out.

At the reception desk, the redhead was gathering her purse to leave too. "Oh, Blackie, don't forget, Miss Zanva's friend called from New York, He wanted her to get the message right away."

Andrea's face lit up in eager anticipation. She really wanted to hear about the contract, Blackburn realized. He felt a strange panic deep inside him.

"Yes? What is it?" Andrea asked.

The other woman glanced at a slip of paper. "He said Shelby Johnson has signed a contract with Boston."

Andrea's breath stopped and the color drained from her face.

"Somebody important?" Blackburn asked when she said nothing.

"No, well, she's a . . . another dancer we know."

"So what's the big deal?" he persisted.

"Oh, it's . . . just good news for her." Andrea added almost inaudibly, "And utter catastrophe for me."

"How's that?" he asked.

She glanced up from her trance, wide-eyed and frightened. She took a step backward, away from him, and looked around in confusion.

He grasped her shoulders to steady her. "Andrea, are you all right? Do you need to sit down?"

She stiffened at his touch. "Of course not. Let's get these other matters cleared up." She pulled out of his grip and stalked past him and out the door. He watched her, then with a shrug he followed.

They climbed into the battered pickup and soon were driving silently across the prairie land. Big difference this time though, he thought. Yesterday she was all in a stew about ditching her car and messing up her clothes but there was a kind of tantalizing warmth between them sitting close in the cab of the truck. Today she was in some kind of stew about the ranch, and that message about the ballet put her in some kind of shock. *It feels like she's deep down in a cold well and I can't reach her,* he thought.

He glanced over at her. She still sat clutching the file folders to her like she was trying to hang on to life. He could almost hear her trembling.

"I know you're anxious to get down to the particulars of your inheritance," he said. Maybe he could ease her into talking about things. "This east valley pasture is kind of unusual. It was a project—"

She snapped out of her reverie and looked at her wristwatch. "Yes, indeed. I'd like to see it, but it's getting rather late in the evening. I hope we can get there before it's too dark."

"Yes, ma'am. As I was saying, the east valley has been kind of an experimental project. Merrick was filing claim on all his surface and groundwater rights a couple of years ago and got interested in a new program out of the soil conservation service. He used the east valley area in what they call a coordinated resource management plan."

He looked over at Andrea. She was listening but with a strained, tired expression. Blackburn continued, "Well, we fenced the pasture into paddocks and installed I don't know how many miles of water pipe and a water storage tank fed by some windmills. You see, the idea is to increase the carrying capacity of the land along with its environmental quality. A lot of people think it's a boon-doggle, that it's too easy to overgraze the land and ruin it. Have your buyers indicated whether they have an interest in continuing the project?"

She looked bewildered. "I . . . I haven't discussed the details with them yet. Everything's still tentative." On the last word her voice weakened into a near sob.

Blackburn stared straight ahead while the pickup creaked and bounced another few miles. Then he stopped in the middle of the road, now a mere pasture trail. He slammed out of the truck and strode a few yards across the prairie. He bent to study the tufts of grass. He cursed to himself.

The woman is driving me out of my mind, he thought. *What kind of person is she? What does she want? What am I supposed to do with her? I hate a complicated woman.*

She'd been a burr under his saddle since he'd first heard about her and for the past two days he'd felt like the bucking and kicking was tearing his guts out.

He heard her walk up behind him and stop a few paces

away. He twisted the long blade of range grass in his hand, trying to calm the pounding in his chest he always felt when they were alone like this. He stood and stuck the blade of grass in the corner of his mouth. It tasted warm and sweet with late-summer maturity. He remembered the warm, sweet taste of Andrea Zanovya.

"Is this the . . . the managed, coordinated whatever?"

Her voice, weak but struggling to be strong, jolted him from his thoughts. Without turning to look at her he nodded and waved an arm at the sloping valley below them. "Yeah, this whole area is fed by the creek and the holding tank at the top of the canyon," he said. "You can see the taller grasses are coming back; riparian vegetation is excellent for this part of the country too."

"Riparian?" she asked, coming to stand close to him. The evening breeze had grown cool and she sheltered herself just behind him at his left.

"All the plants that grow right along the bank of the creek," he explained, his voice coming out too low and gentle. He cleared his throat and went on, "The creek hasn't gone dry since we started."

"No?" she murmured softly.

He wondered uneasily if she was thinking of their morning antics at another part of this creek too. He shifted, scuffed the ground with his boot, blew the grass blade out of his mouth, and stuck his thumbs in his pockets.

Andrea ambled a few steps forward and pointed to the steel-post paddock fences gleaming silver at dusk. "And those are the cattle pens you were telling me about?"

He dared to look at her finally. She stood slim and erect, her delicate profile ghostly pale in the darkening twilight, her sleeve fluttering daintily in the breeze. *Too perfect for me,* he thought.

"It's rather pretty in this light," Andrea said.

"Yeah," he agreed, wishing he could tell her what he felt.

"But why are the cows bunched up in those few pens and not scattered loose across the whole area like they are in the other pastures?" she asked.

He smiled at her genuine interest. "Native plants sprout and mature at different rates so by moving the stock from paddock to paddock every few days, depending on the condition and variety of plants available, the cattle can eat their fill of the young, tender plants," he explained eagerly, falling into step beside her as she walked down the hill.

"There is a very real danger of overgrazing, of course, and that's why there's a lot of opposition to the idea. So each paddock has to be left fallow more days than it's grazed, but the result can be a better, thicker ground cover." He was talking rapidly now, trying to get all the information in before the mood was broken.

"Merrick had a lot of success with it. His calf crops improved, weaning weights and stocking rates increased, and there's even a little wetland area developing down the creek there." He pointed to the south, then realized it was too dark to see it.

"If all you're telling me is true it sounds like a very innovative, environmentally correct, commendable project, Mr. Blackburn," Andrea said.

"The old man had high hopes for it," he replied simply.

She stopped and turned on him with a flash of anger. "Then why were you so secretive about it? This morning why did you act as though you didn't want me to see it? Why had you never mentioned it before at all?"

She moved in close and planted herself right in front

of him. She looked up, not at all intimidated by his towering frame. "Just why have you been so irritatingly cagey about absolutely everything, Mr. Blackburn?"

He grabbed her by the arms, trying to remember not to break her, and slowly, with all his frustration and impatience trembling in his voice, answered. "Because, Miss Zanovya, I promised Merrick, your father, to do my kindest and most careful best to get you to come to Mantilla Bluff. So maybe you'd learn to love it enough to take a little time away from that cursed career of yours to let the other half of your heritage have a place in your life!"

Even in the moonless dark he could see a glint of light reflecting from tears in her eyes.

"My career is over."

Chapter Eight

He still clutched her shoulders, almost lifting her feet off the ground in his strong grip. The enraged determination in his face melted into bewilderment. *Poor cowboy*, Andrea thought. *He's always lived the life of his dreams; he could never understand the major life-changing blows I've endured today.*

The pressure on her arms eased and she was tempted to collapse against his comforting bulk and cry out her misery again. But she didn't have the energy. She simply stood motionless and leaden and let the tears flow silently down her cheeks. Despair and hope, denial and certainty had battled in her mind, but when she said it she knew.

"My career is over," she repeated.

"The guy that called you at the office?"

"Yes, I guess I forgot to give Nigel the phone number at Mantilla Bluff," she said. She couldn't believe she was being so calm about it.

"That Shelby person? She got the job you wanted? Are you sure?" He sounded genuinely concerned, and that touched her.

She nodded and stepped around him. It was difficult finding her footing on the uneven ground but she had to keep moving. "I'm sure," she said. "Shelby and I have danced in many of the same companies. She's very good and we've competed for roles before. We have a lot of traits in common. We're the same body type, same coloring, same energy, same strengths, same weaknesses.''

Blackburn strolled near her, listening silently.

"Shelby danced with San Francisco last season and had a really good year." She chuckled mirthlessly. "I had a really good season too, but if you have a Shelby Johnson you don't need an Andrea Zanovya. We're interchangable parts. And I guess it's her turn to dance 'Giselle' in Boston. Not mine.''

They had reached the paddocks and Andrea stopped to lean against a metal railing. "You know, I think I like these beasts better with a big metal bar between us," she joked. The animals were dark masses in the night, snuffling quietly and moving little. It was serene here and easy to talk in the cloaking blackness.

Beside her Blackburn bent and leaned his muscled arms on the top rail. She couldn't see his face under the brim of his hat. She remembered how frightening his presence had been yesterday and thought how odd it was that his presence now was somehow comforting. Even after all the tension that had passed between them.

"Well, that's just one part in one company," he said. "Sign a contract with someone else. One setback doesn't end a career if it's that important to you.''

"Yes, I suppose I can do that," she said. "I probably will do that. But it won't be the same thing.''

She pushed away from the fence and walked on. "This was my big moment, my breakout role. The chance of a lifetime to prove myself, show everything I can do. And now I've lost it.''

"Won't there be other chances? Other important roles? Other big moments?" he asked, following behind her.

"I don't know," she said, fear and frustration coming out in her voice. "I really don't know. Timing is important in a dancer's career. I'm ready now. My technique is crisp; my body is disciplined and ready. Before I came to Texas and let my life get scrambled, my mind was focused and ready.''

She wheeled around to face him. ''You don't understand, Blackburn! This was my time. I was going to own that role!'' She broke and ran blindly. Frantic, desperate movement was the only thing keeping her from exploding. The ground was uneven and she stumbled a few times but she kept running until she came to the creek.

Winded, she slowed to a walk. *I have completely lost my mind,* she thought, looking around for Blackburn. First, she stepped on something sharp, hurting the arch of her foot. A few steps later some stones rolled as she stepped on them and she turned her ankle. She caught her balance quickly but not before scratching her leg on something. Then she felt stickers collecting at the hem of her slacks. They felt like needles in her fingertips as she tried in vain to pluck them out. She sat down with a sigh.

I hate the country.

After a few minutes Andrea heard Blackburn approach. She was glad he was nearby, although her pulse raced nervously as usual.

''I know what you're thinking,'' she hurried to say. ''But I'm not a lunatic, really. Or at least I wasn't until I came to Texas. This clean air must be doing something to my brain. I flip from rage to laughter, from determination to frustration. I don't seem to have a very good grip on things any longer.

''I thought this would be a nice, sleepy little house on the prairie and I've never lived through such turmoil in my life.''

"Just a fish out of water, I expect," he said, coming to squat on his heels beside her.

"Yes, floundering and gasping for life," she agreed.

He brushed the stickers off her clothes in a few short strokes.

"Ow, how can you stand to do that?"

He laughed and shook the last few from his hand. "Aw, I've been stuck by worse barbs than this."

There was suddenly an air of loneliness about him. Andrea wondered what kind of barbs he meant. She'd taken him for a simple hired man at first, then found him to be a lawyer as well, with senators and music professors-turned-ranchers as friends. KittyLu had hinted that there was more to be learned about the man. Indeed, Andrea thought, he always seemed to be hiding things and thinking more than he said.

"Look," Blackburn said, "I'm the last guy to be telling someone they ought to quit anything. Lord knows I've butted my stubborn head against many a solid wall." He paused, considering. Andrea sensed that this was more revelation than he usually permitted himself.

"But there comes a time when a strategic retreat is the only way to win. Or to come out alive."

"What do you mean?" she asked.

"Maybe it *is* time for you to make a change. If this Boston thing isn't going to work out and the idea of dancing somewhere else sounds like a poor substitute. If it's gotta be all or nothing. I can understand that, believe me."

The night was silent around them except for the soft gurgling of the creek. Andrea's throat caught as she nodded in understanding.

"Yes, that's the way it is," she said quietly. "I don't mean to seem like a prima donna. It's just that I have earned this chance by a lifetime of study and hard work. If it's to be denied me, then there's nothing else. I won't limp along in a career that never quite reached the standard that was expected of Lorraina Powell Zanovya's daughter.''

"You have another chance. You have another parent to live up to," Blackburn said. "Dolf has given you the chance to see the other half of your life.

"He loved you, but he kept the promise he made to your mother to leave you alone. Since he never heard from you, he thought . . . ," Blackburn abruptly stood and kicked at a rock. "That you had rejected him."

Andrea's heart ached at the thought of an old man spending twenty years waiting to get a call or a letter from the daughter he loved and never knew. "I'm sorry, I'm sorry," she whispered. "If I had known anything, I . . . "

She realized something else then. "You thought I had rejected him too." She scrambled to her feet. "And that I came out here only for the inheritance. No wonder you had such a low opinion of me."

Blackburn shrugged and Andrea smiled. She thought of all the confused events and misunderstandings of the past two days. "Well, I would say this has been a real tragicomedy of errors," she said.

"Yeah, I'm still trying to adjust my thinking to the new facts too," he said, rubbing his hand across the back of his neck.

This could explain those times when she knew he wanted to touch her but didn't, she thought. But it didn't explain the times he *did* touch her.

Her encounters with the man were always so volatile, even before she began suspecting him of hidden motives in the settlement of the estate.

Why? she wondered. Why did he always make her feel off-balance? Men were often interested in her. Just as often, she paid little attention to them. It pleased her to be found attractive to men. She was vain enough to enjoy their advances—except Blackburn's attempted kiss that first time. She had been furious at that. Furious beyond what was called for, she realized.

Why? she wondered again. She tried to find a simple, logical explanation. *Perhaps I instinctively sensed the trouble this trip to Texas would cause,* she told herself. *Perhaps I do have the precise and perceptive intuition a great artist needs,* she mused. *Perhaps Mother was wrong.*

Andrea started violently. *Whatever put that thought into my head?*

"What's wrong now?" Blackburn asked. "You're not going to run off into the night again, are you? I think I'm too tired to chase you very far."

"I . . . uh, it's nothing. I . . . just had the strangest thought," Andrea stammered. She couldn't stop the swirl of ideas and emotions going through her. The shock made her shiver.

Blackburn put a gentle arm around her shoulder. It was warm. He tenderly nudged her into walking along the creek. "My mama always said ladies should never frown; it gives 'em wrinkles," he said.

His deep, soft tone was more than Andrea could bear. She swallowed the lump that had formed in her throat. "*My* mama—mother—always said that study and hard work were what made her a great dancer. That using one's instincts was fine if used very sparingly and only after all other resources were properly employed."

He waited while they took a few more steps, then finally asked, "Huh?"

Andrea let out a small laugh of nervous relief. She felt a warm teardrop at the corner of her eye. She breathed deeply and continued with difficulty, "She told me I had an aptitude for excellent technique and that I should concentrate on that aspect of my talent. She said I had no real instinct or inner sense of artistry. That comment always hurt me, but I never realized . . . until suddenly just now. I never realized how angry it made me too.

"I've been angry for years that she felt I didn't really have her talent and I just now admitted that anger." Andrea slapped the tears away from her eyes.

Blackburn stopped and turned her to him. He lifted her chin to touch her face in the darkness. "Was your mama wrong about you?"

Andrea blinked back tears. She refused to weep over this. She would face it sensibly, as though it were a difficult new dance passage she would have to walk through slowly again and again until she mastered it. But she took the handkerchief he offered her.

"You have a way of getting right to the point, don't you, Mr. Blackburn?" she said. "She was wrong. I *am* talented. I have a gift for dance. And now I think I'm developing an instinct for emotional truth.

"Now that it's too late," she added bitterly. The hot tears came freely, but she kept her head erect.

"And that's what gave you that spasm just now?"

"She was wrong! She didn't believe I had the talent to be as great a dancer as she was and that hurts me. And I *am* an artist. I am! But now I've missed my chance and I can never prove it and I'm sorry. And I'm angry!" Her fury came out in huge, gasping sobs now.

"Why did she do that to me? Why didn't she teach me how to develop that instinct? Why didn't she let me use my emotions?

"Why didn't she tell me about my father?"

Blackburn wrapped hard, comforting arms around Andrea and stroked her hair. "I don't know. I don't know why she never told you about Dolf. Back then some folks thought it was better for children if they just made a clean break and forgot about each other when they divorced."

"Divorced?" Andrea lifted her head in surprise. Through her tears Blackburn was a smear of brown face and white shirt. "I never knew they were married. I thought—"

"You mean you thought . . . ?" Blackburn squeezed her to him as his laughter belted through the night.

A sound choked its way out of Andrea's throat. "I thought I was a . . . a bit of an embarrassment." She wiped the tears from her eyes and burst inexplicably into giggles. She wrapped her arms around him and they laughed together. Relief flooded through Andrea as quickly as the tears had coe. She laughed harder.

She still questioned her sanity. Andrea had always kept her emotions firmly in check and well below the surface of her calm exterior. And now those emotions had changed mercurially many times since she had stepped off that plane in Amarillo yesterday.

Had it only been yesterday? So much had changed since then. Especially Andrea Zanovya. She became aware of Blackburn's form pressed against her. She had clasped herself to him naturally and it felt so right she hated to break away. She hesitated a moment more, memorizing the breadth and strength of the man, then pulled back.

"You seem to know as much about my mother as I do, or more," she said.

"He talked about her to me a lot," he said. "I guess they were an odd pair of lovebirds. Everybody around here was crazy about her. My mom used to call her a madcap. 'Course, they thought a lot of him and would have loved anyone he loved.''

"I can't imagine Mother living here or married to anyone but Father . . . the father I always knew," Andrea said. They fell into an easy pace once again.

"Dolf was a good old man. I wish you had known him," he said.

"Tell me about him. All I know is that he was a rancher who rolled his own cigarettes and a professor of music at the conservatory where my mother studied."

"He was quite a musician. Played with Arturo Toscanini when he was just a young boy," Blackburn said.

"No, really? Gee, he must have been old."

Blackburn removed his cowboy hat and pushed his hair back the way she had seen him do before. "Yeah, he had quite a distinguished career in music before they came back here. You'll see all the clippings and stuff when you clean out the house.

"I guess him being a professor and her just a student caused a problem at the college. That sort of thing just wasn't done in those days."

Andrea listened earnestly, eager for insight into this chapter of her mother's life. It was like hearing a romantic fairy tale, not a real story of the woman she had known.

"They married and he had to leave the school. He'd always planned to come back here anyway, so he was happy to come, but your mother . . . " Blackburn fumbled with his hat "Merrick said she felt like she was being banished to the wilds of West Texas before she even had a chance to see if she had any talents to use."

Andrea's heart surged with sympathy for her young mother, just out of school and ready to explore the world of ballet. "I can imagine just how she felt," she said.

"I have pictures of her early career. She was fresh, eager . . . incandescent."

"My parents used to talk about the good times they had out here." His voice sounded defensive. "They had to work hard but they played hard too. And raising families was important too.

"Dolf said he just about went nuts when he heard you were on the way. The day she told him he bought you a pony. Raina—that's what he called your mother—threw a fit, but he said he'd have you riding before you walked."

Andrea shook her head. These people who were her parents sounded like charming strangers. Would she ever really feel the connection with these events and this place?

"Ah, the stories he used to tell about you as a baby." Blackburn chuckled. "I guess you were persnickety back then too."

"Oh, please," she protested. "This I don't need to hear, especially from you."

He grinned. "I've even seen pictures of you buck naked."

"No. They didn't do the bearskin rug thing, did they?" she asked.

He laughed and nodded. She laughed too, and walked ahead of him for a while. She noticed the sky seemed lighter.

"What time is it?" she asked him.

"The wee hours," he answered, "so your reputation's ruined."

"We haven't been out all night, surely." She had been on such an emotional roller coaster she couldn't focus on real time.

"Naw, it's just moonrise," he said easily.

"Now that tells me precisely what time it is," she said. "How far have we come from the truck?"

He grinned again. "A few miles, but we're home anyway."

They walked over the next rise and met the moon hanging low and yellow over the horizon. The house was a few yards away down the slope. The moon lit their path now. Andrea noticed tables and chairs stacked on the patio. "What's all this?" she asked.

"Probably started getting ready for the barbecue while you and KittyLu were out shopping," he said. He opened the unlocked kitchen door and let her precede him.

"I love the way everyone comes and goes so casually around here. It's like owning a hotel." Andrea said, frowning and blinking as she flipped the switch and the sudden flood of light over the familiar room jarred her back to reality. She hated to lose the cozy intimacy she'd been sharing with Blackburn in the dark night. It wasn't often she could be so open and vulnerable with another person, and the end of the mood made her realize how tired she was.

They stood in awkward silence for a moment, then Blackburn said, "Well, it's late."

"Yes," Andrea replied, struggling to think of the right thing to say. "Uh, I kept you from your dinner. Shall we see what we can find in the refrigerator?"

His smiled kindly and his deep brown eyes seemed to understand. His tenderness frightened her. Andrea turned away. This tall, rugged male knew more about her fears and failures than any other person and, while she was beginning to trust him, she didn't want to need him.

While she scrambled eggs and heated leftovers he disappeared into the back room and returned with a small box of old photos. They ate at the kitchen table and

Andrea studied snapshots of her mother as a young woman with a distinguished-looking middle-aged man with a dark, bushy mustache. He was tall and had a commanding air, but a genial smile. There were a few more of the same man, much older with a white, bushy mustache. She wondered whether he had been soft-spoken, gentle, quiet or perhaps quick, brash, jovial.

"The cowboy classicist. He looks like quite a character," she mumbled, swallowing a mouthful of something spicy and cheesy. "There's a twinkle of humor in his eyes."

"He was a storyteller," Blackburn said. "Old Dolf could spin a yarn out forever. He liked having people around, liked to laugh, liked to work hard. I think it like to have killed him when she lit out."

Andrea watched him while he spoke of the old man. Blackburn really cared about him, she thought. He didn't let himself care deeply about many things, but when he did feel something he must have been formidable in its defense.

He caught her studying him and she looked down at her plate. "This spicy dish is excellent. I was starving," she said.

"I noticed you didn't eat much at lunch," he said. Andrea glanced up at him. Was he teasing her about Rachel? She looked away before he could read her thoughts.

"But I guess you dancers get used to eating like birds."

"On the contrary, we burn up so much energy every day that we can eat anything we like," she said. Then she thought of losing the contract and wondered what she would do with her life now.

"Did Merrick ever tell you what made her leave?" she asked.

Blackburn leaned back in his chair thoughtfully. "That's something only Dolf and she knew for sure. But I took it that the ballet just lured her more than the life here. She just felt she had to try her original plans before it was too late."

Andrea could understand that; her mother had been gifted and to deny that gift would have been unthinkable.

"But why did he never contact me?" she asked. "He kept up with my career. Surely after Mother was gone he could have—"

Blackburn rose impatiently. "He promised not to contact you and he kept his promise. It wasn't right, but he kept his word."

"So he left me this ranch to make a connection with me while still keeping his promise to Mother," Andrea said.

"It was important to be able to give you something. Even if you wanted nothing to do with him, he thought you might care for Mantilla Bluff."

Blackburn leaned down and looked gravely into her eyes. Her skin tingled at his touch when he gently placed her hand in his rough one. "Make Mantilla Bluff your home now," he urged. "You want a new life? Here it is. It'd be different from the one you've had, but aren't you a different person now too?"

His voice was low, a coaxing whisper. "This is a good place to be free, to find yourself, to create who you want to be."

Andrea spoke softly too. "You make it sound so very tempting, Mr. Blackburn."

"I mean to."

"I don't know if I could make that big a change."

"Can you go back?"

"That's the one thing I am certain of—my life will never be the same." Andrea laughed ruefully.

She stared down at the big, tanned hands stroking hers. They were work-roughened, but lean and graceful too. His touch always made her pulse race with expectation and fear of her own response, but this time she was receiving strength from it as well. It almost made this idea of his sound plausible.

"I'd be leaving all my friends behind," she said at last.

"You've got dozens of new ones here already, just waiting to get to know you," he replied instantly.

"I would be leaving everything familiar. I haven't exactly acclimated myself to the conditions of living in the country very well so far," she said.

"It's easier than learning to live in the city, believe me."

She noted the look of regret that crept into his expression. "Are you speaking from experience?" she asked.

A cloud of wariness darkened his brown eyes. He dropped her hand and turned away. "Yeah," he said. "I did my time in the culture capitals."

He turned back to her, forcing his mood to change. "But, hey, Perico's getting all the latest hallmarks of civilization—video rentals, cappucino cafes, suntanning parlors. Though why a body would need to tan indoors in West Texas is beyond my comprehension."

Andrea laughed and rose to gather the dishes. "Then there's the language barrier. Is there a Texas-to-English dictionary to explain words like 'persnickety' to me? And all these strange expressions and metaphors you people use?"

"You're a smart girl. You'll pick it up." He helped her clear the table. "Next objection."

"I think Senator Keith might have a strong objection to my taking up permanent residence at Mantilla Bluff."

He looked down at her as he reached up to a cupboard. A devilish gleam lit his eyes. "You gonna let it stop you?" he challenged.

Andrea felt the violent heat as her face flushed. She froze in place, not knowing how to respond. Her throat constricted and the pounding of her heart echoed in her ears. *How does he do this to me?* she thought. He stood very close to her, shading her from the kitchen light. She could smell his woodsy, leathery scent and almost feel the crispness of his shirt.

Her gaze wandered from his mesmerizing eyes down the angles of his face to his firm mouth. She felt her lips part. Finally, she answered, "No."

Chapter Nine

Andrea slid her hands up his chest, feeling the crisp smoothness of his shirt and the firm washboard muscles underneath. Reaching his broad shoulders, she grabbed fistfuls of his shirt and pulled him down to her. This time she wasn't accepting his kiss or responding to his kiss, she was *commanding* it. He gave readily, pressing her back against the kitchen counter and breathing fire into her. She loved the teeming energy in the man as he crushed her to him roughly and tangled her hair with his caress.

Her heart seemed to have stopped beating and she had the same whirling sensation she felt when pirouetting rapidly across the stage—an airborne, weightless freedom. But this time she wasn't solo, she carried with her a solid rock of dangerous masculinity.

She pulled her mouth off his, gasping for control. "You take my breath away," she whispered close to his cheek. "Give a girl a chance."

"You started it," he said between nibbles on the side of her neck.

She shivered with each press of his lips. "I'm suffering from . . . emotional shock and . . . sleep deprivation, so I . . . can't . . . be held responsible for my actions."

"I was afraid of that," he said, kissing her chin, nose, and eyelids, "but what's my excuse?"

She kissed the depression at the base of his throat. "I have several theories. You're a prisoner of your lust—"

He vibrated with a low chuckle. "Warden, take me away."

"Or," she continued, nuzzling his neck, "you think Yankee women are easy."

She felt him stiffen. He gripped her shoulders and pulled back to look at her sternly. "I don't," he said. His dark eyes glowered worriedly.

She met his gaze steadily. "I know," she said. "I think it's just that you're as crazy as I am."

His look softened; he laughed and tousled her hair. "I think you're right."

He stepped away from her and looked around for his hat. Something inside Andrea screamed *No, no.* in protest. If he left her she feared she would explode. In all this impossible, insane day this was the only thing that truly made sense, she thought, and that really didn't make sense.

Her thoughts must have shown on her face, for he looked down and fumbled with the crease in his hat. He thought about something for a moment then he shrugged nonchalantly and reached out a hand to brush Andrea's cheek lightly. "You need to get some sleep," he said. "You look beat."

"How considerate of you to say so," she said, leaning into his caress.

His eyes twinkled with humor. "I want you to be well rested for the barbecue. I'm gonna teach you how to do some real dancing tonight." He hesitated briefly as he gave her mouth one last look, then he walked jauntily to the door.

Andrea wondered how he could be so energetic when

she was so exhausted. "Sorry I took you so far away from your truck," she said.

"No, you're not," he tossed over his shoulder as the screen door slammed behind him.

Andrea laughed and watched his tall, muscular form as he trotted out of sight behind the house. She still felt that mystical bond that existed between them, as if their pulses beat in the same rhythm.

When she was in his presence every sense was heightened by that bond and she was alternately frightened, confused, or overwhelmed with a sense of exciting possibility. When he was gone it always took her a while to catch her breath and come back down to earth. Yet he always remained with her in a sense too.

Since she had first watched in alarm as he slid out of his truck in dirty, tattered work clothes and ambled toward her when she was stranded on the highway, she had known this man was a dangerous force she'd never before encountered. Back then she was thinking of physical danger and, later, of business opposition. But now she knew this force was an even greater peril—the electricity created when two opposites attract, when two storms converge.

Was this how Mother felt? Andrea wondered. Was she facing the same choices?

Her mother and Merrick had met on a common ground at the conservatory. Andrea was in Blackburn's world, a world far different from her own. When she met Merrick, her mother hadn't yet had a chance to try her wings, whereas Andrea could look back on a proud and satisfying career. She understood her mother much better now. She could empathize with a young woman's need to realize her artistic potential. Andrea had that same need. She could sympathize with the woman's single-minded, hard-driving discipline too. Giving up the man she loved had been a high price to pay for her art; she had to make the results worth it.

Andrea now knew her connection to this place and was beginning to accept the altered history of her life. Still, the change was revolutionary, leaving the city and the world of dance to live on an isolated ranch among people whose lives were centered around other ideas. Could she do that? Would she be able to make it work?

"Did I actually say I was staying in Texas?" she asked aloud and the irony of it hit her. "I hate Texas . . . I think."

Andrea had left a note on the refrigerator asking Esperanza to let her sleep late. Apparently she had slept blissfully through a morning of hubbub, for when she looked out her window a half dozen women were setting up the long tables on the terrace, spreading tablecloths, and anchoring their corners to keep them from blowing in the breeze. She pulled on jeans and a blouse and added a jacket to dress it up. She brushed her hair hurriedly and went downstairs to see if she could help. The dining room and kitchen were filled with dishes of food, utensils, plates, and all kinds of picnic supplies.

Espy and two other women were wrapping flatware in napkins and arguing over where to place flower arrangements. "There won't be room for them on the tables," Espy said.

"But the wind will tear them up if we put them around the edge of the dance floor," said another woman Andrea remembered meeting in Perico yesterday.

"Not if we wait till sundown to move them over there when the wind dies down," said another woman. She looked up and smiled at Andrea. "Hi, I'm Lois Moore."

"Hello," Andrea answered. "I'm sorry I'm getting such a late start. What can I do to help?"

The women smiled approvingly and handed Andrea a tray of utensils to sort.

The ranch was a carnival of activity all day. Each arriving family brought food or an ice chest or a case of pop to add to the feast. The men began an elaborate operation of cooking even more food on outdoor grills and setting up lights and hanging decorations. The women decorated the tables and arranged and rearranged the dishes on them. Even with dozens of children running and playing everywhere Andrea couldn't imagine the house and terrace holding enough people to eat all the bounty.

Each new arrival also brought more introductions, condolences on her loss, and heartfelt thanks for holding the barbecue. Andrea had little time to think about her nervousness at seeing Blackburn again. The bustle and excitement around her made her eagerly anticipate the celebration in spite of her recent worries. The guests easily and informally accepted Andrea as one of their own, chatting and joking as they worked.

Once while she climbed a ladder to adjust a spotlight over the dance area it occurred to Andrea that she felt stronger and more in control of herself than she ever had. She felt at home.

KittyLu arrived in late afternoon wearing a bright-orange Mexican dress embroidered with blue flowers. She clanked with heavy silver and turquoise jewelry as she introduced her husband, a pleasant, graying man who said little. *Probably out of practice,* Andrea thought mischievously.

KittyLu's little girls raced up and clasped Andrea's

hands. "See, Mama, Andrea's wearing jeans too," Tiffany said.

"Well, she's been workin' but she's going to be a lady and change into a dress for the party like I was trying to get y'all to do," their mother answered. "But no, I got two cowboys for daughters."

The girls wore boots, jeans, western shirts, hats, and even small bolo ties like many of the men wore. "And you look very chic," Andrea told them, hoping she wouldn't be pulled apart by their enthusiastic attentions.

"Scat, you two. It's time for Andrea to put on that pretty dress we bought yesterday." KittyLu swatted the girls out of the way and steered Andrea toward the house. "We need to do something with that hair. I want you to look fabulous tonight."

"Why, KittyLu? What are you up to?" Andrea asked.

"Me? What could I be up to?" She grinned and fluttered her heavily mascaraed eyelashes. "Oh, honey, you are going to be the absolute center of attention tonight, what with the traditional Merrick barbecue and everybody wanting to get to know you and wondering if you're gonna sell the place to Rachel."

Rachel. Andrea had mercifully forgotten about Rachel. She would be here tonight. Andrea felt queasy. Rachel would be here, fawning all over Blackburn, trying to buy Andrea out, generally making her feel threatened and unsure. *KittyLu is right*, Andrea thought. *I have to look fabulous.*

She showered and changed while KittyLu described the people who would be attending and reviewed the main events of their lives. She obviously relished imparting information. "You'll just see all kinds of things comin' to a head at the barbecue, not the least of which will be

Rachel Carswell Keith's latest campaign to get Blackie interested in marryin' her,'' she said.

"Latest campaign?'' Andrea asked, trying to sound casual.

KittyLu shook her head and her dangling earrings moved more than her hairdo did. "She's been sniffing after him since we were kids. And just you watch, she'll be dogging him the day long. And I wouldn't be surprised at what else she'd do to get him.

"I don't understand it but she can twist any man around her little pinkie. Any man but Blackie—so far.''

Andrea felt herself growing heated and angry at the thought of the two of them together. She remembered Rachel's possessive air and her hands on Blackburn's shoulder, arm, face. She suddenly wanted to touch him again, reassure herself of the sincerity of his feelings for her, to push Rachel out of his mind. She whipped her wet hair off her face and said, "Mr. Blackburn doesn't seem to mind her attentions.''

"And that has always just vexed me to the core,'' KittyLu said. "You know, I wonder if that big offer to buy Mantilla Bluff isn't some kind of angle to bring those two together. That witch always wants it all.''

She frowned and pondered this possibility.

Andrea was jerking her clothes on much too roughly for the delicate fabric. "What about Blackburn?'' she asked.

"What about Blackie?''

Andrea sat in front of the vanity table and, with effort, unclenched her teeth. "What does he want? Rachel?''

"Shoot! I imagine he's had all of Rachel he could possibly want, if you know what I mean.'' KittyLu raised a knowing eyebrow at her and started combing Andrea's hair.

"Oh? They have a history together?"

KittyLu huffed. "To hear her tell it. Rachel and Blackie have always had a kind of understanding but not in the usual way people mean when they say that."

For once, Andrea was glad her friend was a nonstop gossip. If she kept silent and nodded occasionally, KittyLu would tell her everything she knew about Blackburn and, remarkably, she was sticking to the subject.

"It was like they brought out the opposite in each other," KittyLu continued. "Rachel brought out the wildness in Blackie and he brought out what little good there was in the girl. You know what it reminds me of?"

KittyLu waved the hair dryer at Andrea's reflection in the mirror. "There's that scene in 'Gone With the Wind,' my all-time favorite movie, where Scarlett says somethin' like she wants Ashley's heart and he says 'You have my heart, you cut your teeth on it.' That's like them, close in a way but not a good match."

She considered that, then shook her head. "Well, 'cept I like Scarlett a lot better than Rachel and Blackie's not as big a wimp as Ashley and Rachel never really wanted Blackie until she got out in the world and realized what a great guy he is by comparison.

"But to answer Your question, no, I don't think Blackie really wants anything he doesn't already have. Or had once. That's kinda sad when you think about it. It shouldn't be. I mean, he seems to be contented and he certainly has plenty to do with his ranch and his law practice and all the things he does for people. But still, it seems kinda sad to get so near to what you truly want and then lose it."

Andrea tried to sort through the maze of KittyLu's comments. Was Rachel trying to rekindle something from their past? Was their "understanding" an ongoing relationship? Was there a marriage being postponed by Rachel's political career? Blackburn certainly hadn't behaved like a man planning to marry someone else, Andrea thought.

She jerked her head with the sudden awareness of where her thoughts and actions were taking her. She was actually considering giving up her dancing career and moving to unknown territory—that was crazy enough. But not only that, she had let her emotional impulses allow a physical involvement with a man she'd met two days ago. And now she was yearning to destroy his close relationship with a woman he'd known all his life.

She fidgeted in her seat, fighting the logical explanation of why all this was happening.

KittyLu released a strand of her hair from the curling iron she wielded and patted Andrea's head. "I didn't brand ya with the iron, did I, honey?"

"No!" Andrea said too forcefully. She was telling herself she wasn't in love. Not with some cowboy who laughed at ballet and snarled at all things urban and "Yankee."

"No, no," she repeated more calmly, pushing the worrisome thoughts from her mind. She examined the soft, loose curls KittyLu had created. "You're doing a wonderful job. I didn't think you could . . . uh, it's lovely."

With grave concentration KittyLu took up her instruments again. Andrea let her work in silence for a minute, then said casually, "Blackburn doesn't seem to spend a lot of time at his law office."

"Well, my Henry is the senior partner—does most of the paperwork. But they both keep busy," KittyLu said absently.

"I guess ranching is Blackburn's main interest. His life's ambition, would you say?" Andrea asked.

"Life's ambition?" KittyLu said thoughtfully. "No, Blackie had worldwide ambitions at one time. He was some big muckety-muck with the government. Traveled all over Europe for a couple of years."

"Really?" Andrea asked in amazement. "Mr. Blackburn gives such a different impression. I was surprised to learn he'd even been to college and law school."

The fear began to build in her again. Everyone had secrets to keep from her.

"Oh, yeah, he hobnobbed with all the famous foreign people." KittyLu nudged her knowingly. "You know what I think? Personally, I think Blackie was a spy. 'Course, you'd never get him to own up to it."

Andrea laughed. "But you're getting your analogy mixed up," she teased. "Rhett Butler was the spy, not Ashley."

KittyLu was unperturbed. "Yeah, and he got caught too, didn't he? A nice, mild-mannered gentleman farmer spy like Ashley—or Blackie—might have more success, don't ya think?"

Andrea laughed again at the wild idea and turned to view herself in the full-length mirror. KittyLu was right, she thought—she did look fabulous in the floating folds of gauzy white fabric. The bright colors of the Spanish motif and her recent days in the sun made her hair and complexion glow warmly.

KittyLu beamed proudly. "You are gonna knock 'em outta the saddle tonight," she said.

Dressing up made Andrea want to join the party. Mysteries and disasters could be forgotten about for a few hours, couldn't they? She fastened a large, fresh gardenia in her hair and gave KittyLu an affectionate hug, a gesture she never would have felt comfortable with before.

Senator Keith's legislative aide stopped at the bottom

of the stairs as she descended. Will Campbell whistled softly and let his gaze travel from her legs to her face in frank appreciation. Andrea smiled at his boyish flirtation and squeezed his hand. "You flatter me, Mr. Campbell. I'm sure working everyday with the stunning Senator has made you quite a connoisseur of feminine beauty. And you include me in that high regard?"

"Top of my list," he answered. "And, by the way, she's just my boss, okay? I'm off duty tonight."

Realizing Will could provide just the information she needed about Rachel's motives, Andrea said, "No shop-talk? I was hoping you'd tell me more about that toxic waste project I've heard about. Your work is so interesting."

Will looked at her in disbelief. "Now who's trying flattery? Shall we dance or should we eat before you start talking about toxic waste again?" he said as he led her outside.

There were dozens more of her rural neighbors and Perico residents milling about the yard. A mariachi trio played a lively accompaniment to the greetings of how nice she looked and how glad everyone was the barbecue went on as scheduled and how old Dolf would have liked it. She found herself asking the older people how they had known "her father" and eagerly listening to their reminiscences. Once during a story about Merrick doing fieldwork for the federal soil conservation service Andrea caught KittyLu watching her. KittyLu smiled and gave her a quick, approving nod.

"So old Dolf sent Washington this requisition form for a hundred new cattle guards," a beefy cowboy continued, chuckling and anticipating the punch line to the story. "Some bureaucrat sent back a letter saying he looked it up and saw that they already had more'n three thousand cattle guards in the state and why did they need to *hire* a hundred more? How many cattle did they have and how many guards did it take to watch 'em?''

The storyteller pushed back his straw cowboy hat, exposing a pale forehead over a sun-reddened face that exploded into gales of raspy laughter along with his listeners. Andrea wasn't quite sure what the joke was, but she and the small Gonzales child in her lap laughed with them anyway.

Will Campbell found her again and pulled her away from the group. "Enough of the hostess bit. Let's eat; the food smells great. Have you ever had real, old-fashioned Texas barbecue?" he asked without waiting for a reply. "Homegrown, corn-fed beef, slowly baked underground by hot coals. Ah, it'll melt in your mouth.''

"Yes, I saw them taking the beef out of the pit and I really thought it must be some kind of joke on the city girl,'' she said.

Will fed her a bite of the succulent beef that was just as he described. Ladies filled her plate with vegetables, salads, and tortillas. Each woman had a favorite recipe she wanted Andrea to try. Will steered her to the front of the house and they dined at a bench under a huge cottonwood tree by the stream. When they had feasted and she felt she could work it comfortably into the conversation Andrea once again asked about the legislative committee on toxic waste.

"Yeah, there's been some traffic of waste products coming into the state that hasn't been carefully regulated and the Senator's committee is about to close off the loopholes. It's causing people to scramble; waste managers are getting their dump sites bought up and dumpers are getting rid of stuff that won't pass muster after the new law,'' Will said. "Why all this interest? You in the waste business?''

"Oh, no,'' Andrea said quickly, trying to sound casual. Then she decided to test his reaction to a direct question. "I know some prospective buyers are interested in this ranch as a waste dump site because of its remoteness and geographical features. I wouldn't want to sell to them without being sure that it's a safe waste site.''

She watched him lean toward her carefully and gently dab at the corner of her mouth with his napkin. Andrea stirred uncomfortably at his nearness.

"A little sauce,'' he explained. Andrea reached up to move his hand but he cupped it under her chin. He leaned close and gazed lovingly into her eyes. "Let's just have fun tonight and solve the environmental problems another day.''

Andrea looked around self-consciously, knowing his attentions to her would be fuel for speculation. No one had noticed—except Blackburn. He stood across the terrace glowering at them.

She had glimpsed him through the crowd at times earlier in the evening laughing and talking with friends and neighbors, his baby-blue western shirt and bronze skin setting off that wide grin that occasionally flashed across his face. He seemed to be avoiding her just as she had avoided him. Her inner radar warned her each time he came near and she shied away from encountering him in the presence of so many people. The feelings they shared last night were dangerous and new to Andrea. She didn't know how to act toward him, especially in public view.

Apparently he had felt the same, for he avoided her too. Now his full attention was focused on her and it was an angry, threatening concentration.

Andrea fought an urge to flee that swelled inside her.

For the last two hours she had been feeling whole and calm for the first time since she came to Texas. Now he was walking toward her through a crowd of friendly people and Andrea felt trembling panic.

She steadied herself, lifted her chin resolutely, and said to Will, "Take these plates away, will you please? Then we can dance off some of these calories."

Will saw the look that passed between Blackburn and Andrea but said simply, "Sure. Be right back."

Blackburn was at her side. "Gettin' pretty friendly with ol' Will all of a sudden, aren't you?"

Before she could reply a syrupy voice that Andrea hated interrupted. "There you are, darling!" Rachel slid up to Blackburn and attached herself to his arm. She had on a sophisticated gray suede outfit, understated and expensive. She looked at Andrea's dress, arched a questioning eyebrow, and continued, "Blackie, Daddy was asking after you. He just never gets to see enough of you, darling. We'll have to find some way to remedy that, won't we?"

As Rachel pulled him away the setting sun caught Andrea full in the eye. Its late-summer brightness hurt her eyes. She closed them tightly and turned away. *I hate that woman,* she thought. *I really do.* Why did he put up with her? How could he stand her unctuous, cloying manipulation? There had to be something between them. There had to be.

Will was at her side again, questioning the look of disgust that must have showed on her face, "What is it, pretty one?"

"You men! I just don't understand how you can be the way you are."

He looked in the direction Rachel and Blackburn had gone and smiled. "Maybe you just need a little closer study of the species."

He put his arm around her waist and pulled her toward the bluff. The mariachis had been replaced by a country-and-western band and a dozen couples were dancing on the flat rock floor below the sheer face of the outcropping. Mantilla Bluff was once again glowing fiery orange in the sinking sun. Will swept her into an unfamiliar dance. After a brief awkward moment she quickly picked up the steps and swung and glided easily over the rock with him.

The music and the steps were lively fun. Andrea enjoyed being in her natural element even if it substituted a prairie rock for a stage. She loved dancing in any form. She loved floating with the music and using her slender, graceful body for communication. She had often thought she could express herself better, even think better, with her body in motion.

Will was a smooth, able dancer, but Andrea found herself wishing it were not his slight frame pressed against her. She wanted to be in Rachel's place. She often caught sight of the two of them across the crowded dance floor.

She liked seeing the way Blackburn moved. His pale, crisp shirt was pulled taut across the sun-bronzed muscles of his chest. He had a grace and lightness in his powerful step that surprised her. *No, it shouldn't surprise me,* she thought. *It's the same when he moves in to kiss. It was the same when he chased me through the creek.*

"What is it?" Will asked.

"Hmm? What is what?" Andrea brought herself back to the present moment.

"You were miles away. Or was it just a few feet away?"

"What do you mean?" she asked innocently. "Guess I was just concentrating on my dancing. It's an occupational hazard with me."

"Yeah?" he said and twirled her farther away from

Blackburn and Rachel. "My friends will never believe I spent the evening dancing with the famous Andrea Zanovya."

"Shall I autograph your dance card?"

Will smiled seductively and pulled her closer. "Don't have a dance card. You'll have to give me something else to remember you by."

She pulled back and replied, "You'd do better to wait until I'm really famous, wouldn't you?"

Just then the music stopped, they stopped spinning, and she saw Blackburn across the crowd again. He had another scowl on his face, yet there was something else in the look too. It wasn't the worried impatience that she had seen so frequently. It was something vulnerable or. . . . It was jealousy! Andrea couldn't repress a slight smile.

She was unable to resist giving Blackburn a taste of his own medicine, and besides, maybe Will could give her some information on the toxic waste site. "Will, let me show you around my ranch."

She hoped that Blackburn saw her leading Will around to the front yard. The twilight was deeper on this side of the house. Children were playing down at the creek bank. Their squeals and laughter floated up and blended with the dance music coming from the back. Will turned her around to face him and tried to embrace her. Andrea pulled away gently and sat on the bench made of twisted juniper. Will sighed and sat down beside her. "I didn't think so," he said.

"What?"

"I didn't think you really wanted to get me alone so you could take full advantage of my charm," he said.

Andrea smiled, embarrassed. "I . . . uh, thought you

might have some information about the toxic waste proposal for Mantilla Bluff.''

He sighed impatiently and chided, ''It's the weekend, Andrea. Time for all good government bureaucrats to leave their desks and have some fun.''

''I don't mean to be a pest, but I need information I can trust.''

Blackburn's imposing figure loomed at the corner of the ranch house. The sight of him automatically filled her with apprehension and confusion. She couldn't sort out the reaction she had to his appearance. Warmth and yearning vied with worry and mistrust. She was sure of only one thing, that she had to do something to exorcise these demons.

She leaned into Will and kissed him lightly on the cheek, saying ''well, thanks for the dance, anyway.''

Andrea slid out of his reach before he could respond. She floated off into the night, the delicate folds of her white dress fluttering and swishing about her knees as she moved. It made an attractive sight for both pairs of eyes that followed her.

Chapter Ten

Andrea kept her composure until she rounded the corner of the house. Then she ducked into the sheltering shadow of a large lilac bush, gasped for breath, and tried to calm the violent trembling inside her.

Have you lost your mind completely now? she asked herself. *What could you be thinking? You're at a barbecue and hoedown on the Texas prairie caring about a man who is still a virtual stranger.* Even considering a relationship with a cowboy had to be the most insanely impulsive thing she had ever done.

She rushed out of her hiding place. She had half-hoped Blackburn would follow her. She listened for sounds behind her while she searched the crowd on the patio and the dance floor.

She had to keep moving; she could think better with her body in motion. She walked near the edge of the brightly lit area. The party was livelier than ever now that the purple dusk had darkened into night. Several families with young children were preparing to leave. Andrea distractedly said good night to them. She wanted to rush back to where she had left Blackburn and Will, but she was afraid to return the way she had come.

She decided to go through the house and get a peek at what was going on. Women were still replenishing the food tables from the bounty in the kitchen. KittyLu spotted her. "Well, I told you you'd cause a ruckus tonight, didn't I?"

"What do you mean?" Andrea asked quickly.

"That Will Campbell sure has monopolized your time. Should we put out more desserts or more of this calico salad?"

"Both," Andrea replied. She had become used to KittyLu's intertwining patterns of thought. While KittyLu nodded and picked up a dish Andrea slipped through the quiet house and into the seldom-used front entry porch.

She peered out on the black expanse where she could barely make out the figures of the two men. It really would be horrible if they came to blows over her and she had to admit, she would be to blame. She knew none of this was fair to poor Will, who had no idea what was going on. Suddenly, there was a rumble of male laughter and Blackburn slapped Will on the back. Will nodded and walked away.

Andrea jumped nervously when KittyLu stepped up close behind her and looked over her shoulder. "Well," she said, "your two beaux seem to be getting along right nicely."

Andrea sighed in relief. "They certainly do. Right nicely."

Andrea wrenched open the door and walked over to Blackburn.

There was what seemed to be a long silence between them. "Will and I go way back," he said slowly, adding meaningfully, "we know each other pretty well."

Andrea couldn't see his face but she knew he'd seen through her subconscious attempt to make him jealous.

"I don't have to defend your honor," he continued. "You can take care of yourself." A teasing grin slid across the shadow of his face as he added, "When you want to."

"Blackburn, you are impossible!" she exploded, dismayed at how he could almost read her mind.

He laughed, obviously relishing her fit of pique.

"Oh, you're really enjoying all of this, aren't you?" she fumed.

"Yes, and so are you."

Andrea doubled up her fists, wanting to punch him in the face. But she pushed her fists against his chest and giggled instead. She was glad he couldn't see the blatant emotion she knew was evident in her face.

She shook her head in exasperation. "What's happened to us? For two people who started out with so many mistaken ideas about each other, we certainly have gotten painfully honest with each other, haven't we? Where did we go wrong?"

He chuckled deep in his throat. "Come on, I promised to teach you how to dance."

He led the way toward the noise and music. When they reached the first dim spill of light she could see that he was frowning in concentration. He paused without turning to look at her. "It's really about trust," he said. "Not just in the person but in the thing you feel between you."

They were standing no closer than casual acquaintances. He hadn't touched her at all, but Andrea felt as close and intimate with him as she ever had. She said nothing, allowing him to gather his thoughts and continue.

"I've played the games before," he said. "All the testing and proving yourself and . . . well, I'm not going to play them again."

His frown was stern, his voice low and gentle. "You got to have faith in the feeling," he said almost as if he were understanding it for the first time himself. "It's there; you trust what you have together or there's just no use fighting."

Andrea realized that, in this jumbled explanation, the man had revealed to her more of his soul than he had shared with anyone in a very long time. He was beginning to open his own feelings to her just as she had shared her most private torments with him. She marveled at the deep, mutual confidence that was building between these two strangers—and polar opposites, she thought with a smile.

At the dance floor, each reached out a hand to the other and they moved easily into the flow of a two-step.

"So KittyLu tells me you were a spy," she said.

He looked down at her with a sly, drowsy smile. "Dang, my cover's blown."

He added a swift spin to the step that swept her halfway across the floor and caused her to gasp a quick breath. She felt light-headed and remembered she'd felt the same breathless sensation when he first kissed her. He held her gently and guided her steps with slight pressures from his hand at the small of her back and, she imagined, from the sheer force of his will.

He remained casual and offhand, changing tempo and step handily as the music changed with each dance. They spoke little but laughed a lot as Andrea learned the Cotton-Eyed Joe, the schottische and several lively line dances. She could tell she impressed him with the way she quickly picked up the steps and kept pace with him as he tried to challenge her by adding nuances and complications. Finally, winded from dancing and laughing, he took her to the patio for a break.

"Come on," he said, "you're exhausted from all my teaching."

"Me? Exhausted? I can still dance rings around you,"

she said, tapping out a short time-step on the terrace stones.

"Aw, here." He shoved a glass of iced tea into her hand. She laughed and eased gratefully into a chair. She was used to dancing for hours at a time, but not on solid rock. Her calf muscles ached more than she would ever let him suspect. He hooked a boot heel against the wall of the house and leaned back comfortably.

She accepted compliments on her dancing and Blackburn exchanged nods and small talk with the others roaming around the food tables. Andrea could read the speculation in their faces and was surprised to find that it didn't embarrass her. This whole Texas thing still seemed an unreal adventure to her. Tomorrow everything would get back to normal. . . . But normal wasn't normal anymore either, she thought.

KittyLu approached her carrying a plate with a huge slice of confetti-colored cake. "I want you to try my Orange Rainbow Fiesta," she said. Even KittyLu's food was bright, Andrea thought, staring at the sugary mound on her plate.

"There's another use for your carbon dioxide," Blackburn said.

"What?" Andrea looked up at him then at their surroundings. "Now I know that thing uses carbon dioxide," she said, pointing at the fire extinguisher near the barbecue pit. "But Orange Rainbow Fiesta?"

He nodded. "Cake mix. They use carbon dioxide when they blend it."

KittyLu's head bobbed up from where she worked at the table. "Cake mix?" she said indignantly. "Blackie, I have never used a cake mix in my life. I make everything from scratch. The very idea."

Blackburn grinned and winked at Andrea. He reached

for a can and sprayed whipped topping on her cake. "Carbon dioxide is used in some pressurized containers," he said, trying to sound like a boring teacher.

"Sure, professor," Andrea said, placing the fork and her plate back on the table.

He stabbed a fork into a sliced tomato and held it out to her. "Carbon dioxide is used by commercial growers to ripen tomatoes for market."

Andrea rolled her eyes. "Yeah, right. And for aspirin and Coca-Cola."

She pulled him back toward the music. "You're not as good a liar as I've given you credit for," she said.

"I've never lied to you," he protested.

They had reached the edge of the dance floor. She turned and looked questioningly at him. "Oh?"

He looked away and shrugged. "Just never quite told you everything all at once."

She gasped in astonishment but let him put his arm around her as they started to dance.

"Okay, okay," he said. "Most of the carbon dioxide produced here is used in enhanced oil recovery." After a moment he added stubbornly, "But all that other stuff too."

She laughed and tried to see if he was actually blushing. She couldn't quite tell in the flickering light and shadows of the bluff dance floor. The smile faded from her face and she said seriously, "I believe you."

He glanced down at her briefly and looked away again. They were dancing another two-step, then the music changed into a dreamy, lilting waltz.

She was tentative in his embrace. The fingers of one hand lay lightly in his palm and her other hand brushed his shoulder. His firm jaw hovered near her face as they moved. She could feel the warmth of it and smell the fresh-air scent of his cologne. Each time a wisp of her hair touched him she felt a charge of nervous electricity. She was almost afraid to touch him and aching to at the same time.

The demure space he had left between them felt like a question to Andrea. She took a deep breath and, at the next turn, moved closer to him, relaxing cozily in his arms. His grip tightened and she closed her eyes and leaned her forehead on his chin. She found that when she pressed her left thigh against his she could anticipate his next step before he took it and follow his lead without a moment's hesitation. They moved as one, as part of the swirling pulse of the music.

Andrea wanted this feeling to go on forever. She would never tire, never hunger or thirst, never need or want anything but this sensation of warmth and care and belonging. Smiling dreamily, Andrea finally dared to look up at him. She slowly admired the strong lines of his face until she came to his eyes. They held a curious look of wonder and fear.

As the music stopped Blackburn released her and glanced around self-consciously. "How about something to drink?" he asked.

"Yes, that would be fine," she said and gave him a confident smile. She wouldn't worry about his reaction of discomfort. After all, he said one has to trust one's feelings.

He went off and Andrea sighed contentedly as she strolled toward the terrace. She saw Rachel speaking to a group of guests. Orating was a better word—or pontificating, she thought, judging by the senator's familiar gestures and haughty command of attention. Filled with new confidence, Andrea decided to ask the woman point-blank whether her committee was planning to allow a dump site in the area and what effect it would have on Mantilla Bluff.

She joined the group on the terrace and boldy interrupted Senator Keith's speech with her question. She received a politician's nonanswer. "This state is mighty big country," Rachel said. "We have a great many industries utilizing the very latest of new technologies. If we are to grow economically and to prosper well into the next century, we must accommodate these industries realistically."

"Is that a 'yes'?" Andrea asked impatiently.

Rachel lifted her chin and stood straighter, giving Andrea a cold look. "Miss Zanovya, you of all people, being a sophisticated New Yorker . . . ," Rachel began. There was sarcasm in the term and she knew the woman meant to indicate that Andrea was an outsider too ignorant for her to bother dealing with seriously.

"And being a professional, even if it is in the arts," Rachel was saying in that disdainful tone, "you can understand the importance of keeping people working and keeping the community healthy and prosperous so that it can afford a rich and diverse cultural life. You must agree that is important, I know."

"Yes, Mrs. Keith," Andrea countered, knowing Rachel hated the term of address. "But what I'm trying to find out is—"

"Texas, and this district that I represent in particular, is a place that looks to the future as it maintains a prosperous and vital—"

Andrea stepped closer to her and looked directly into Rachel's eyes. "Do you want to buy Mantilla Bluff in order to make it a toxic waste dump site?"

The cool contempt in Rachel's gaze instantly hardened into anger. Andrea didn't falter even as she heard an expectant hush fall over the group of onlookers. She was no longer afraid of being intimidated by people like Rachel nor of unusual situations like this where she wasn't sure of herself. She had been hit by too many jolts lately to be worried about causing a scene or about confronting information she didn't want to hear.

Rachel glared at her. Andrea had never experienced the hatred that was directed at her now. It was frightening to see, yet somehow it exhilarated her to know she had destroyed the senator's oily confidence. Rachel's voice quavered as she replied, "I am buying Mantilla Bluff to . . . to ensure that it continues to be the fine example of Texas agribusiness that it has been for generations."

She labored to take a breath and regain her composure. "As for these other wild environmentalist suspicions of yours," she said, turning to the crowd and shutting Andrea out with a smirk and a knowing look, "why, you just drop by my office on Monday. My staff will be happy to take the time to answer any questions you might have about agricultural chemicals and fertilizers and such things."

Andrea wasn't going to let her get away with such a dismissal. She would not be put down as an outsider, a Yankee who couldn't possibly understand the land or the needs of those who lived on the land. Rachel's reaction had told her that she'd hit a nerve.

"Of course I don't know much about ranching," she said. "I never claimed to. And I admit I don't know as much about the environment as I probably should. But I know that there are businesses planning to establish such a waste site somewhere in the region and I know that your legislative committee is responsible for site selection and the regulation of such projects."

She glanced around at the neighbors listening to the

exchange. They understood her implication. Andrea lowered her eyes for a moment, then looked solemnly at Rachel again. "And I know that Adolf Merrick didn't spend his life building up this ranch to see it changed into something else. Even late in his life he continued to look for innovative improvements," she said earnestly. "He wanted the land to be lush and self-sustaining, a place for things to grow, not a place for unnatural poisons. I can't let you, or anyone else, buy Mantilla Bluff unless I can be assured that his wishes will be honored."

Andrea didn't realize that she had made such a decision until the words were out of her mouth. Hearing her own impassioned speech frightened her a little. She was taking responsibility, not only for the ranch, but for an obligation to the old man. She was acknowledging that she owed him something, at least.

Rachel waited to see if Andrea was finished with her pronouncement. Her perfectly sculpted face once again had that look of smooth, cold stone. Her voice was smooth and controlled.

"I grew up not five miles down the road from Mantilla Bluff. I've ridden my horses all over this land. Why, Dolf Merrick used to whittle toys for me. I think I might know as much or more than you do about what he wanted for his land."

Rachel's statement hit Andrea like a wave of icy water. She shivered with the cold shock of truth. Maybe she didn't know what was best for Merrick's ranch, she thought. Maybe she was an outsider who had no right to make any decisions. Maybe her concern for Mantilla Bluff had come too late. But what else did she have now?

Before Andrea could think what to reply, Rachel caught the arm of one of her constituents and started leading him off saying, "That reminds me, Marvin, I spoke to the governor about that matter you brought to me and we both think we've come up with a way of handling the problem.''

Rachel had deftly avoided answering any of her questions and, at the same time, reminded her listeners that Andrea was an uninformed interloper, while she, their hardworking personal representative at the state capitol, had always been one of their own.

Andrea folded her arms in exasperation. She remembered the debate she and Blackburn had had last night in the kitchen when she joked about Rachel objecting to her owning Mantilla Bluff. ''You gonna let that stop you?'' he had asked. And she had answered.

Blackburn's soft chuckle sounded behind her. ''You ever see a sidewinder?'' he asked. ''Smart little rattlesnake that can slither sideways quicker'n you can guess which way.''

''I can't think of a more appropriate metaphor for her,'' Andrea said. ''I'm just surprised you recognize the resemblance and still let her coil around you all the time.''

She looked up and saw that irritating smirk of amusement on his face. ''Or are we talking 'birds of a feather' here? No, what is the snake version of that expression? Shedding skins together?''

Andrea stopped abruptly when she realized the implication of her phrasing. She reeled away from him, angry and embarrassed.

He laughed and stepped close behind her again, placing his arms protectively around her. She could feel their warmth through the thin mesh of her sleeves.

''She's an operator, all right,'' he said, ''but she serves her constituents well enough.''

''I'll just bet. Some better than others, no doubt.''

Blackburn's hands slid up to her bare shoulders and

stroked lightly. Andrea's breath caught and as she released it the tips of his fingers tickled her skin.

The sound of his voice pierced the light-headedness she felt. "You worried about it?"

Andrea couldn't move. She almost couldn't speak. "Uh, the band is leaving and so are the rest of the guests."

"Throwing me out again?" he murmured close to her ear.

Andrea coaxed her body around to face him and saw Rachel approaching once more with Blackburn's hat in her hand. Andrea bit her lip to keep from telling the woman how ridiculously predictable she was. "It seems you have prior commitments," she said and shrugged away from him.

"Darling, it's time to say good night," Rachel purred. "I hate being the last to leave. We're usually the first."

Blackburn looked uncomfortable and Andrea was glad. He looked doubtfully at Rachel. "I should help clean up," he said. "Make sure the yard lights and torches are out safely. Chairs stacked."

Rachel looked around with distaste. "Yes, I suppose we really should help clean up."

You've never cleaned anything more than your pretty face, Andrea thought. But she smiled sweetly and said, "You run along. I can take care of Mantilla Bluff myself."

Rachel's eyes glinted a message but she said nothing.

Blackburn scowled at her as he accepted his hat, then pulled keys out of his pocket. "Okay, saddle up."

Andrea saw guests off, convinced Espy to leave the rest of the night's tidying to her, promised KittyLu to phone the next day, and finally had the vast ranch to herself again. She was tired but restless and couldn't make herself go inside the house. She checked the ashtrays a final time and turned out the brightest lights.

She walked back to the rock that had served as a dance floor. It really was remarkable, she thought, such a smooth, even surface. Just perfect for an outdoor gala. Right below the bluff with the lights making its rough white face reflect more light back on the dancers. Andrea leaped through a quick jeté and arabesque in the golden light.

"Ugh." She groaned aloud as she felt a quadricep twinge. The sound of her voice seemed oddly small in the quiet night. *It's no wonder I'm exhausted,* she thought. *Can't dance on stone, you idiot. I hope I haven't ruined my muscles.*

She looked up at the bluff. There was just a whisper of balmy breeze in the warm night. A green scent flavored the air, something soft and sweet.

The sky above her was the deepest, darkest blue Andrea could imagine and it was strewn with stars, More sparkle than she had ever seen in the city. There were so many stars she wondered if they cast a light themselves. She flicked off the bluff lights. There was no moon, but her white dress glowed in reflection of what fragments of light remained.

What a glorious place Mantilla Bluff was, she thought. She could understand how a person could love it so much he never wanted to leave it. Her mother did leave, though, she remembered. She had other dreams to fulfill. Her father stayed and filled his life with hard work, friends, and private pursuit of his love for music. A good, satisfying life from all reports.

Andrea twirled again and her skirt floated out in a soft circle in the vast, dark landscape. But what a lonely life it must have been for him too, she realized. Thinking of her mother and she so far away, living without him. Why did he let them part?

Andrea understood her mother better now, after her conversations with the neighbors who had known her as a young woman. What she had always interpreted as her mother's single-minded devotion to dance Andrea now recognized as a driving need to affirm her life's choice. Andres Zanov had been a good husband and a good father to Andrea, but now she saw that their only real bond was a love of ballet. Even their parenting, training Andrea for the stage, was a part of that bond.

Andrea shook her head. But Mother was a great artist, she thought. She was destined for the dance. That couldn't be explained away as just a substitute for love. She was gifted. To ask her to abandon her gift would have cheated a wonderful woman.

Why did life have to be so complicated? Andrea thought sadly. Why didn't people just stay where they belong, away from troubling entanglements? Why did they fall in love with the wrong people? *Why did I come to Texas when I should have been in Boston seeing to my career?*

I've lost my life!

She had to move. She had to get away to an unfamiliar place. She just had to be someplace different, somewhere not twisted up in the memories of the past few days here and not a part of her previous life. But there was no place to go.

Mantilla Bluff loomed unperturbed behind her and in the distance tree branches formed a tangle of black, barely distinct from the blue darkness of the night surrounding her. She could hear the faint gurgling of the shallow creek below. It was all part of an impossible future that she knew she wasn't ready to face. Anywhere else was a part of her past that was now painfully lost to her.

I won't cry, she told herself. *I will not succumb to emotion again.*

There was a soft scuff behind her. She wheeled around.

Blackburn's shadowy outline came around the edge of the bluff. "Came back to help you lock up," he said.

His silent, stealthy appearance alarmed her just as it had the first time she had seen him on the deserted highway. "How did you get here? I didn't see your truck."

"Drove up behind the bluff. That's the shortest way from Rachel's. Thought I'd leave it on the far side where it wouldn't be seen." He turned his head. "People talk."

He seemed to notice that she had shrunk back and wasn't moving. "Did I scare you that badly?" he asked.

"Uh, no, I—" she mumbled as she looked toward the house. He reached for her but she flinched away.

"Why, Andrea?" he demanded. "Why are you so skittish?"

"Because you . . . I'm not . . . I have things to do."

She moved toward the patio. He followed and caught her by the arm, pulling her around to face him. His angry scowl looked fierce in the dim light that came from the house. "You know I wouldn't do anything to hurt you, don't you? I'd never force something you didn't want."

Andrea didn't speak. She couldn't. She had nothing to say that would make any sense to him. Nothing made sense to her. Pieces of her life kept disintegrating in front of her eyes. She was powerless to stop it and she was unable to stop the fear it brought.

Blackburn released her arm but stood motionless where he was with his face close to hers. "We've locked horns since you first got here," he said. "But there were other times too.

"I thought those other times maybe earned me a little of your trust."

"Trust?" she whispered. "Why?"

She could feel his lips almost touch hers.

"You feel something special and new and incredible for me, I know it," he said. "You can deny it all you want to, but I know you do."

Chapter Eleven

It's true, Andrea thought. *Heaven help me, it's true. I hate his deceit but I love the touch of his hands on my skin. I hate the mysterious blanks in his life but I can think only of being with him.* She closed her eyes and breathed in the sensation of his nearness.

Yes, she thought, *I do feel something new and incredible with you. But it might destroy me.* It took all the force of her will to pull away from his lips. She looked up hopelessly. There were still enough party lights to illuminate his face as if in candlelight. His expression was a mixture of tenderness, fear, and resolve.

She understood that conflict and spoke to it. "This is impossible. I've just lost what I spent my whole life working for. I don't belong here, as Rachel so kindly pointed out. I don't know the man who was my father. I can't get any answers from my mother. I can't be the person I intended to be. I can't sell the ranch. I can't stay here depending on you for help for everything. I don't even really know you."

The truth of her last statement hit her. She began to tremble. "I don't really know you and here I am contemplating a complete upheaval in my way of life, to live here and be near you and only have the barest inkling of who you are and what you're like and why."

He shook her, trying to stop the torrent of words. "Andrea, listen to me."

156

"Listen to what? Listen to your kind explanation of why I inherited this ranch? You really handled that bit of news intelligently, didn't you?" She pushed angrily against his chest, crumpling his shirt in her fists. It was the first time in her life she had felt truly violent toward another person.

"Andrea, I had to let it happen like he wanted it to. He wanted me to handle it his way so you could see what kind of daughter you wanted to be to him."

"What difference could it possibly make after all this time?"

"All right, get mad," he said calmly. "Spit nails. You're entitled. But is it me you want to beat up?"

She released him and with a furious swish of her skirt moved away from him again to the edge of the terrace. She realized he was right. Her anger was misplaced and it was more fear and rebellion than hurt. Once again he had read her heart better than she could herself, and the violent emotion drained out of her, rendered harmless by his plainspoken understanding.

He reached her side. "I know there's a lot of explaining to do," he said quietly.

She laughed feebly and shook her head. He embraced her gently. She smelled the warm summer night and leaned against his chest where she had crumpled his shirt. Something ached in her chest. She almost couldn't form the words. "This relationship of ours is ridiculously impossible, isn't it?"

He didn't blink or change the tenderness of his gaze. "Yes," he answered.

"And you're not going to explain it to me?"

"No."

Her heart felt leaden. "What am I to do?" she asked softly as if to herself.

"Trust it, anyway. Just for tonight," he pleaded. "Just for tonight, risk believing in me because you want to. Now, before the moon comes up, while you look so beautiful, just forget everything your common sense tells you and dance with me."

He began to waltz her around the terrace between the crowded tables and out to the shadow of the bluff. She let herself be drawn away. Let herself be possessed by the bond that was between them. Yes, she thought, perhaps for just an hour she could forget all her doubts and suspicions. She couldn't really trust anything, but she wanted to be in his arms again . . . for just a little while.

He held her close and their bodies swayed and spun as one in natural harmony. She had never been partnered so well on the stage.

"There's no music," she said.

"Wicked, isn't it?"

Andrea threw her head back and laughed. She let herself look up at him and drink in his closeness and the delight she felt. She felt safe; it was so dark perhaps he wouldn't see the love and longing in her.

His smile faded into hunger. His lips touched hers lightly. She leaned into the kiss just as he pulled back suddenly.

"What time is it?" he asked. "Can you read my watch?"

She squinted at it in the darkness, puzzled and sorry he had interrupted the moment. "It's two-forty or three-forty. I'm not sure."

"Come on, it's almost time." He pulled her around the side of the bluff.

Andrea was alarmed. "What? What is it?"

"You'll see." He scrambled up the sloped side of the bluff, pulling her roughly behind him. Just as they came over the top he pointed to the opposite side of the hill. "There," he said.

She looked at him. His expression was that same mixture of delight and anticipation she had seen when they toured the ranch. He drew her up beside him and put his arm around her waist. She followed his gaze just as the full moon burst bright and honey-colored over the far edge of Mantilla Bluff.

The sight was spectacular indeed. They watched silently for several minutes. When the orb had fully cleared the horizon and began to pale, Blackburn sighed deeply and grinned at Andrea. "Now that's entertainment," he said.

She smiled, cradled his face in her hands, and kissed him with all the passion she had been afraid to feel. "I thought you had finally gone as crazy as I am."

He shook his head and kissed her neck. "I did that the day I saw you fighting the mesquite barefooted."

"I was quite attractive, wasn't I?"

Kisses went down her bare shoulder. "When did you fall for me?" he asked, tracing his fingertips just above the neckline of her blouse.

"I haven't." She tried to make it sound like a joke. "I can't. You're a liar and a spy, maybe some kind of villain."

His fingertips went reluctantly down her arm to her wrist and fingertips. He stepped away from her and she felt as though part of her own body had left with him. He walked across the top of the bluff, thinking and scuffing the ground with his boot. The moon lit the landscape with a ghostly glow. She had spoiled the mood and she wanted to recapture it, but the truth kept creeping into their relationship.

"You're mighty logical for an artist," he said at last.

"I thought dancers were supposed to believe in romance and feelings more than dull, stupid things like facts."

Andrea heard the sorrow in his voice. "Well, there is the school of thought that stresses technical perfection first, only supplemented by passion and instinct," she replied.

He looked at her questioningly.

She answered the look. "Technique has always come more easily for me."

"But it's the other part that I need from you."

Andrea wanted to run to him and swear undying love and perfect happiness. Why didn't she? she wondered. Why couldn't she? Was it really the result of a lifetime of methodical training? Was it really her questions about his past? She had, after all, decided to give him these few minutes of trust.

Or was it something else? Was it what she feared most? Was there some basic flaw in her? Did she lack true emotion in her soul? Was she incapable of feeling the passion he sought?

No, she had to be wrong. *Prove me wrong, Blackburn,* she silently begged. *Come to me and prove me wrong.*

He stared at the still shrinking moon.

Andrea knew this was a pivotal moment in the performance of her life. The few feet of prairie between them seemed like a great expanse. Could she cross it? She had spent her life training her body to respond to her instructions. She willed her foot to move forward and her spirit to follow.

A step from him she hesitated. "What's that sweet scent?" she asked. He knelt and picked a tiny, pale twig.

"Sage," he answered as he held it up to her.

She took it and breathed in its fresh pungency.

"Tell me who you are," she said.

He shook his head and pulled her down beside him. "Not tonight. Tonight all we need is a warm moon, a white dress that feels like cotton candy, and the smell of prairie sage."

Andrea giggled as she melted into his embrace. "What a line. I've always heard cowboys were poets at heart."

"I have been known as a silver-tongued devil in my time," he said with a smile. He cupped her face in his strong hand. "But that's no line. It's the truth. I need you like I've never needed anyone in my life. I haven't really wanted anyone in a very long time. Not like I want you. You stir a passion in me that I thought died a long time ago."

"Please don't say things like that," she begged. "I'm afraid I'll believe you."

"Believe," he whispered, then his lips touched hers with fire and yearning and she was lost in the light of a Texas moon and a cloud of sweet sage. Andrea knew she would forever after think of this moment when she smelled sage. She would know for the rest of her life that she was a creature of deep, primal longings. No matter what happened tomorrow or the rest of her life, she would know that she possessed the fervor required of a great artist—or a real woman.

He dreamily studied the texture of her gauzy dress. "This feels like it would melt in my hand," he said hoarsely. She smiled at his childish delight. He looked as though he had discovered feminine softness for the first time. "I like this dress. You look good in it."

Understated but sincere, she thought, and because it was so simply put she valued the compliment. "Thank you," she said softly, relaxing against the rough turf and stretching her arms over her head to glory in the star-spangled sky.

"You feel good in it too." He leaned over to kiss her again, another long, possessive kiss. Andrea wanted time to stand still. She wanted to be here forever, never to have to think about anything else again—just experience this one perfect moment in time.

"You're getting cold. Better take you in."

"No."

"Moon's almost down." He rose and pulled her to her feet.

"I don't care," she said, slipping her arms around him and resting her head on his chest. She dreaded the feeling of separation from him.

He grabbed her hair and pulled her head back. "Woman, you are temptation itself." His mouth took hers again, eagerly and completely. He pressed her to him, tense and trembling with his own emotions.

"I don't want to leave this place," she said at last. She felt childlike in her pleading, but it was liberating. She no longer strived to be the controlled sophisticate as she had for so many years. She was living the giddy youth she had forfeited for discipline. Her whole line of thinking had been wrong. This was it. This passion, this exploring the vitality of life, was what would make a great dancer. "I don't want to break this magic spell."

"Don't worry, it's unbreakable," he said, but there seemed to be a veil over his eyes now. Her heart leaped with a stab of worry but she willed it quiet again, silently repeating, *Trust, trust*. He took her hand and strolled to the edge of Mantilla Bluff where they stood side by side surveying the endless pastures. The prairie grasses shone silver in the moonlight.

It seemed they could see the whole ranch from here. "This place is magnificent," she said in admiration.

"Beautiful in a stark way. Three days ago I thought it was just treeless. I see so much more now."

He turned to her and raised his eyebrows in surprise.

"Oh, give me a little credit," she said to stop any comment. "I may be a city slicker but I'm not immune to the charms of the wild west."

She was going to embarrass herself without his teasing, she thought, and pushed on. "So, Mr. Blackburn, you were raised out here but left for college and law school and a career in government service?"

"My friends call me Blackie."

"It's a stupid nickname and I hate it."

He chuckled and tried to pull away. She grabbed his arm. "Oh, no, you don't slide out of it that easily. Gee, you would make a good spy. You'd never let anything slip. You never even answer a direct question.

"Now, who are you and are you now or have you ever been a spy for our own or any other government agency?"

He laughed heartily and Andrea loved the deep vibrations of it echoing through her as she leaned close. He clicked his boot heels and bowed slightly. "Agent Blackburn, loyal citizen, farmer, rancher, attorney at law, agronomist, and former agricultural liaison for the United States Department of State, Eastern Europe division. Very minor rank, I assure you."

"Agricultural liaison, huh?" she said, eying him skeptically. "Sounds like a perfect cover for spying. What was that other word?"

"Citizen?"

"No, agron-something."

He laughed again, obviously enjoying her game. "Agronomist—specialist in the chemical constitution of soils. In other words, I'd go to these other boring minor-rank bureaucrats and we'd talk dirt."

"Sounds fascinating. If it's true," she said, giving him a knowing look. "Whatever made you leave it all behind?"

He shrugged casually and looked out over the horizon but Andrea could see the change in his expression even in the dimming moonlight. She kept her voice light and teasing. "Oh, I see, a woman. Some slinky Mata Hari type, no doubt."

"Nah," he teased back. "She was just like you—a beautiful, snobbish Yankee who thought civilization stopped at the city limits."

"I am not snobbish," she said, "and I have grown to deeply appreciate . . . you think I'm beautiful?"

The left side of his mouth twisted into a half smile. "Don't you?"

She laughed lightly. "No, I'm okay. But certainly not beautiful."

He gave her a narrow, piercing look, trying to see if she was being coy or sincere. The look changed briefly to relief and then to a voracious yearning as his gaze traveled down her body. "You're beautiful," he said decisively. "I'm glad you don't know it and I'm glad I'm the one who gets to tell you."

His lips barely feathered across hers in a promise that made her breathless in anticipation. His fingers lightly traced down her neck and shoulders, building a chill in Andrea that flamed into heat when his hands stroked down her back and pressed her to him. His mouth came down on hers with a release of fierce longing and Andrea returned the kiss honestly and eagerly with her own need for him.

Blackburn arrived late at Mantilla Bluff the next morning. He knew half the party guests from the night before would show up to help with the cleaning and he wanted to be sure to give them time to arrive first, and to give Andrea time to . . . to what? he wondered. Recover? Get ready to face him? Fend off any nosy questions?

It wasn't that he was afraid to see her again. No, in fact, it would take an effort to be around her and not to act like a new puppy wanting attention. He laughed at himself. He wanted to see her, all right. He wanted his skin to be touching her skin for about six weeks before they let go.

She had danced with him like she was part of him. She had laughed with him, at him, at herself. They already had private jokes together. She was sharp, clever, quick. He liked that. She was flirtatious, but shy sometimes too.

She had a temper, of course. He'd seen her fly off the handle more than once. He smiled, remembering Andrea in the ditch at the side of the road, Andrea spouting off at him for one thing or another, and best of all, Andrea taking on Rachel.

She would have made the old man proud, he thought with a pang of regret. But she was here now and she was going to stay. *We've watched sunset and moonrise together. And she's made me start living and breathing and wanting again.*

His old truck groaned to a stop at the bluff. Several others were parked around the patio. Espy, Marcy, and their boys were cleaning and covering the barbecue pit. He walked up to them and offered to help. Espy nodded toward the house and said, "She got some company."

She looked kind of serious so Blackburn went on in the kitchen door. Lois Moore and her mother were washing dishes and they looked up and smiled wisely at him as he passed through. *I was afraid of that,* he thought. *It must be written all over my face.*

Andrea, KittyLu, and three other neighbor women were in the living room. Andrea was standing by the fireplace and turned to look at him as he walked in. He always felt this electric jolt when he got near her and it was like she knew he was there before he was. She was wearing those soft slacks and shirt that sort of glided over her shape as she moved. She looked so good and tempting it took him a minute to realize Andrea was jittery this morning.

Then he saw who was making her nervous. A slim, pale man in a business suit was standing beside the fireplace ignoring the others and talking rapidly to Andrea. "It's just what we've been hoping for, 'Drea dear," he was saying.

Blackburn hated the way he mispronounced her name. And the fact that he was here and making Andrea nervous suddenly scared Blackburn.

"You have 'Giselle' and several other plums, Andrea!" He was shouting like she was deaf. "Boston Ballet is offering you a star's contract. You'll dance at least two other principals during the season. Can't you just die? Rehearsals start next week, so I came to whisk you back just as fast as I can. All this inheritance stuff is wrapped up, isn't it?"

Andrea pulled her attention away from Blackburn and back to that guy. "Uh, no, as a matter of fact, Nigel. Good morning, Mr. Blackburn," she called to him.

Blackburn couldn't move. This guy was talking about Andrea's ballet stuff and about taking her away and Blackburn was having trouble getting in the door. Thank goodness KittyLu was there to get in the middle of everything, he thought.

"Blackie, guess what? Big surprise," KittyLu said. "Andrea got that big contract with the Boston Ballet that she was hopin' for. Isn't that excitin'? But I just hate it that she's got to leave right away. Who knows when she'll get back this way again."

Blackburn felt like he'd hit a wall full force. He struggled to draw air back into his lungs. KittyLu was fluttering nearby. Andrea smiled wanly at him. She appeared calm but Blackburn could tell she was poised and ready to rocket off in an instant.

He strode across the room, nodding at the ladies and offering a hand to the man. "Blackburn. 'Mornin'. " he said.

The guy belatedly shook his hand and said "Uh, Nigel Saunders."

Blackburn turned his full attention to Andrea before the man could say anything else. "Well, congratulations," he said. "And you thought that other girl beat you out."

She looked up at him, her eyes full of fear and wonder. She inched away from him. "Yes, it seems Shelby and I are no longer competitors. I can't believe I have exactly what I had hoped for. I just can't believe it."

Blackburn fidgeted with the hat in his hand. *I can't believe it either,* he thought. He remembered how relieved he was when she said her career was over. It had made him feel like a snake because she was hurting so bad, but it sure helped convince her to stay at Mantilla Bluff. And last night when she got mad at Rachel and said that she wouldn't sell the ranch he wanted to shout victory right there in front of everybody.

Now he just felt like a little kid getting cheated at the carnival. He should have listened to the warning signals that kept going off. He kept hearing them and shying away but then kept coming right back to her where he knew there was danger. He was a fool.

KittyLu crossed over to put a protective arm around Andrea and said, "I know this Boston thing is wonderful and important, but I don't see why they can't wait a week or two on you. You wanted to rest. You need some time to set your roots down here. And there's still so much more to do at Mantilla Bluff."

Saunders spoke for her. "Rehearsals start next week and the business we need to conduct in New York must take precedence over any of this inheritance nuisance."

Blackburn imagined his fist going right through Saunders' facial bone structure.

"Nuisance? Well, I never," KittyLu said with a huff.

"KittyLu, Nigel, please," Andrea said. She ran her hands worriedly through her hair. There were new sun-streaks in the chestnut, Blackburn noticed. It made her prettier. "Just let me think for a minute. The contract, notify Pittsburgh, pack, close the apartment. I have to work out for a couple of days, at least, before I dare show my face in rehearsals."

She looked up at him suddenly. "Blackburn, do you think the Gonzaleses would keep running the ranch?"

"Yes, ma'am," he said stiffly.

So she had decided. She was leaving without so much as a moment's hesitation, without a word to him. All the change of the last few days was no change at all. Her father's ranch, his heritage, meant nothing to her. She was her mother's daughter, bolting off for her own career. And for that wimp.

He had thought she belonged to him now. She was a part of him. She had cussed him and hated him and blamed him and he'd felt the same way toward her. Then together they had figured things out. He had given her the strength to piece a new world together after she lost her old one. And she had breathed life back into him.

Together they were one complete, whole, vital being. Together they could make Mantilla Bluff a paradise. Together, here, they could have everything.

He knew it. Didn't she?

Blackburn had a feeling his heart was going to stop stone dead in his chest. It had only been a living, beating organ for a few days and now it was going to crumble into sand and leave him hollow again. He had a fleeting picture of old man Merrick. So this is how that man had lived for twenty years.

He looked at her. Her eyes were wide and bright with excitement. He put his hat on his head and walked out the door.

Chapter Twelve

His boots hit the flat stones of the patio almost at a run before the sound of her voice registered in his mind. "Blackburn," she called behind him as the back screen door slammed. "Wait a minute. We need to talk."

He halted. His jaw set and with difficulty he held in the rage that was boiling inside him. He cocked his ear to the side to acknowledge her presence, but he couldn't turn to face her.

"I thought we should talk about arrangements for the ranch," Andrea said. Her voice was tiny and wavering. A surge of protectiveness battled with his anger. He wanted to soothe her when she felt fearful and at the same time he wanted to shake her for talking about business when their lives were falling apart.

He nodded toward the Gonzaleses, who stood watching them from the edge of the patio. "Marcy and the boys can take care of everything here," he said curtly. "My office can send you the paperwork. Just leave your address with someone."

She stepped closer to him. "But . . . aren't you going to congratulate me?" she asked.

"You don't need my words. You have everything else."

He took off with long, quick strides. She caught up with him again as he reached his pickup. "You have nothing at all to say to me this morning?'' She sounded embarrassed and hurt now.

Don't make it any worse, he said to himself. He stopped again without turning. He didn't want her to think last night didn't mean anything. He had come over this morning to tell her just how important it had been, how she had brought him to life again after years of careful isolation. He had protected himself from hope and caring but she had forced her way into his prison and dragged him out into the sunlight. These last few days had been the hardest part of his life. And the best part of his life.

But she was the one running off.

He let his breath escape in a sigh. This was a lot more public confrontation than he wanted. He walked over to the base of the bluff where at least they'd be out of sight of all their interested friends for a few minutes. He paced in the shadow of Mantilla Bluff like a trapped animal while he waited for her to join him.

Andrea reached for him and the touch of her hand on his arm seared his skin like fire. He didn't flinch though. He endured it in stony silence, slowly raising his eyes to meet hers. He wasn't sure what he expected to see there but the painful insecurity she was obviously feeling hurt him. It pleased him too, he noticed. At least she cared that much.

She drew her hand back. ''Wow, what a morning, huh?'' she said casually. ''What a couple of weeks this has been.'' She looked at him hopefully. ''Everything keeps changing, reversing. Expectations don't turn out to be . . .''

He knew she was giving him time to explain himself but he couldn't. Or he wouldn't.

She knew he wanted her to stay. She knew what she

meant to him. She knew what he could offer her. She knew what was here for her and she had already made plans to leave. He hitched a boot heel against the craggy face of the bluff and leaned back, miserable in the knowledge that these were the last few moments they would spend together here at the base of the bluff where their lives had changed.

"I know this Boston contract is a surprise," she said. "It certainly was to me. I was convinced my career was over and now it's better than I ever hoped."

She paused again and directed a defiant glare at him. "You know how important this is to me," she said, her voice angry now. "I mean, you do understand, don't you, why I have to leave this way? This ranch has been here a long time—the opportunity in Boston won't be."

Blackburn shoved his hands in his pockets.

"Talk to me, you cowboy!" Andrea shouted. "You have to say something."

His throat was knotted and his chest was heavy. He clenched his teeth and pressed his lips together, then managed to choke out, "There's nothing to say."

"Nothing?" He saw her jaw tremble and she looked away.

"You said it the other night. All that stuff about how important timing and technique is." His voice sounded dull and dead, like it was coming from somewhere far off. "Guess your 'strategic retreat' won't be necessary, after all."

"My what? Oh...yes," she said, remembering. "You said it has to be all or nothing for people like me. People like us."

"And you said your body is ready. I certainly can't argue with that." A bitter half-smile leaked out of the corner of his mouth, making his face feel like plaster cracking. He hated sounding so pitiful.

She blushed prettily. "So you think I'm making the right decision to go to Boston?"

"It's not for me to say."

"But don't you have a preference?"

She's getting back on her high horse, he thought. He used to think how cute it was but he couldn't let himself care anymore. After that mess with Helen he'd sworn he'd never love another woman. And he sure broke that promise when this one came along. He'd been stupid to fall for her but there was no way he'd be stupid enough to beg another woman to stay with him.

She was still looking at him, those big, brown eyes full of outrage and innocence. He had wanted those eyes to be looking up at him 'till they were old with wrinkles all around them.

"If there's one thing I've learned in my long and eventful life, it's that the woman will make her own decisions," he said at last.

She stared at him for so long he didn't think he could stand the strain. He wanted to take her in his arms and crush her to him with all his strength. He wanted to feel her firm flesh and smell her hair and hear her low, soft laughter.

And he wanted her to get out of his sight.

"You ever visit back east?" she asked tentatively.

He shrugged. "We ex-spies have to keep a low profile."

She had reached the edge of the bluff's shadow, the noonday sunlight dancing in her hair, when he spoke.

"Stay," he said.

* * *

Andrea knew she had left her heart and hope at Mantilla Bluff, but she was convinced she had been right going back to her world. It was the only thing she could do. Let him work out his feelings as best he could and let her go on with her life. Each time some tender memory arose to warm her heart, a question accompanied it. Andrea didn't understand how the tender, romantic man she had fallen in love with could be the same indifferent, coldhearted stranger she'd observed.

If only she'd never gone to Texas, she often thought. She would know nothing of this hurt and confusion. She would be achieving her life's dream of becoming a prima ballerina and exulting in every joyous moment. Oh, she was thrilled with her new position and the opportunity it was for her. She was back in the life she had always known and loved, she reminded herself, back to what she knew was her destiny. Back to her familiar canyons of concrete and steel.

The tiny, cramped apartment had seemed eerily unchanged when she returned to New York. Yet it was no longer home. She had become used to the spacious ranch house, she assumed. She welcomed a quick move to Boston. She was surprised at how little she had in the way of material possessions to move. The nomadic life of a professional dancer discouraged one from collecting anything but friends and memories.

Boston was cool and brisk in early autumn and Andrea was glad. She wanted everything to be different from her recent life in Texas. She threw herself into rehearsals and training. The few days away from classes hadn't been kind to her muscles. She'd certainly been active enough on the ranch but she had neglected the basic daily discipline of the barre. Dancers, like athletes, had to maintain form and training.

Nigel teased her about taking on the personality of a prima donna—working constantly, speaking and socializing little with the other dancers, craving perfection in every movement. She didn't explain that this was her only escape from her thoughts and emotions. Constant work and obsessive concentration was the only way to dull the ache. She wanted Blackburn, she needed his loving embrace, and she knew she would never have it again.

She couldn't help wondering what had happened to him. At the worst, he would simply go on being quietly lonely. At best, he would do with Mantilla Bluff what he wanted and have Rachel at his side erasing all memory of other women. No, that was the worst, she corrected herself.

At every thought of Rachel she began to tremble with emotion. She was fired with jealousy. She couldn't have him and that awful woman would. It was those times Andrea would work the hardest—maddest, Nigel called it. She would work and work and think about nothing else from early-morning rising until she collapsed with fatigue at night. Work and sleep were all she wanted. No thinking and certainly no emotion that couldn't be channeled into the ballet.

The weeks of work were beginning to have their numbing, healing effect when she received a fat envelope with KittyLu's return address on it. Andrea shouldn't have been surprised. KittyLu had phoned numerous times but Andrea always managed to avoid her.

During a break in the dancers' "green room" lounge, she slumped on an old sofa and opened the packet. There were several sheets of pink notepaper covered in a wide, looping scrawl, a set of crisp white papers, and a clump of newspaper clippings. The business papers were a copy of Rachel's offer to buy the ranch. Andrea flushed hot with resentment and tossed them into the trash. She scanned KittyLu's indecipherable writing, in purple ink, of course. There was unpunctuated chatter about her little girls, everyone missing Andrea, all the local gossip.

But anyway the dust is settling and we're all eager to hear how you are doing in Boston. . . .

Same old KittyLu, Andrea thought and smiled.

Nigel sauntered into the room. She looked at his slender frame in his soft rumpled cashmere suit and suddenly she hated him. He had been solicitous of her every mood and whim since she had returned from Texas. She wondered if it was her elevated status in their profession or if it was her absence that had made his heart grow fonder. She didn't want to have to think about it.

She stood and marched toward the door. He caught her arm as she passed. His voice was calm and even, as always. "What is it, darling? What has Her Ladyship in a snit today?"

She stopped. "I'm sorry," she said. "I got a letter from KittyLu. All that inheritance business is too disturbing for me to deal with right now. I want you to screen my calls and my mail from now on. I don't want communication of any kind from Texas until well after the 'Giselle' run. Keep it away from me, won't you please? As a friend."

She couldn't look at him but she felt his gaze on her for a long moment. Then he said, "Whatever it is, face it, Andrea. Deal with it. Do it. Sell the ranch or give it away. Confront your feelings about your parents. . . . "

Andrea pulled away from him but he went on, "Talk to him. Confront him. Don't keep leaning on me. I'm not what you want."

She looked up at him, surprised. "Oh, Nigel, don't

start being understanding now. Not when I need your sarcastic detachment more than ever."

He chuckled slightly. "All right. Get to rehearsal. Opening night is just a week away."

The week was an amazingly short one. Andrea worked harder than ever. Rehearsals ran late but her energy seemed to build rather than diminish as her starring debut in the Boston Ballet neared. She was getting press attention and the group's social calendar was filling up as the season's opening galas were scheduled. So many old friends were encouraging her.

The directors of the company urged her to rest more. Rest? She laughed at the thought. Rest wasn't what she needed now. The approach of opening night, the work, the pressure—that was the rest her heart and mind needed. Quiet times alone worried and wearied her. Dancing was restful and fulfilling.

On opening night she was ready. She looked at herself in the dressing-room mirror moments before her stage call. Costume, hair, makeup were all perfect. But more than that she saw a woman who was ready to meet the challenge of her destiny. She was calm and confident. She knew she had the talent, the skill, the preparation, and, most of all, the will for great accomplishment.

She smiled at her image. *Yes, I'm happy,* she thought. *This is the moment I have prepared for and hoped for. It's wonderful. If only I had someone. . . .* She stopped herself. *Don't be ungrateful,* she thought. *I have a whole company of friends and many more well-wishers. And Mother really is a part of this. Perhaps even Mr. Merrick.*

But not the one person she really wanted to share this time of triumph with. Her heart yearned for Blackburn, for the love and understanding only he could provide. She ached with the knowledge that she'd feel this hollowness forever. *That's the way it is,* she told herself. *You make choices your whole life long. This one was the right one for me. Don't look back.*

She turned away from the mirror and continued her stretching exercises. The music and the magic began.

From the moment she stepped onstage, it was perfect. Every movement was fluid and precise. She re-created Giselle that night. With the stage lighting on her face she couldn't see the people in the audience but she could feel their approval. She could feel herself drawing them through the story. They were in harmonious communion with her and the company.

As she danced there was a surge of electricity in her veins. Inexplicably she focused on the stage-left side of the house. She stared in that direction and wondered why. She caught one glimpse of a gleaming white dress shirt in a sea of evening wear, then poured her concentration back into her performance.

She was dancing better than she ever had. She had more feeling and more expression with each step. That electricity coming from stage left, whatever it was, carried her to rapturous heights. She had done it. She was living her cherished lifelong dream. She was a true artist.

The set and the performers became a blur of color, form, and motion. She ached with sorrow when the music ceased and she had to stop moving. She became aware of a thunderous noise. The applause. They loved it. They did. Andrea felt light, numb, suspended above reality in a sparkling moment of bliss. She dipped slowly and gracefully into a bow of gratitude.

Someone was patting the perspiration off her face and neck with a fresh towel. There were hugs from every direction and congratulations. She was led back into the lights. Their brilliance flashed and magnified through her tears. A bouquet was pressed into her arms. Such a sweet, hothouse scent.

Finally, the noise was muffled as the curtain closed and the company crowded around to hug and chatter. Andrea thanked them again and again, smiling and gasping for breath after her rigorous work. It was a glorious fatigue. She was completely, happily exhausted. Every fiber of her body sang with consuming accomplishment. She felt like a warrior victorious after the direst battle. She had performed with perfect precision.

More than that, she had infused her dancing with pure emotional truth. She had danced better than her training. She had become the artistic creator she had never dared hope to be. She knew, and the world knew, that she could have a career that crowned and surpassed her mother's achievement.

And in that instant, amid the first flush of triumphant congratulations, Andrea knew she would have the courage to make the decision her mother had not. She could walk away from the stage and all that it held for her. She couldn't live a life apart from the man she loved, the man she was destined for.

Then she felt that strange spark again. She turned to see Blackburn striding toward her in his familiar, confident manner. He had been one of the first-nighters and he looked completely natural and comfortable in studded shirt and tuxedo. The stark contrast of crisp white and satiny black set off the weathered tan of his face. She remembered her first sight of him in worn, dusty jeans and laughed.

He smiled at her in wonder and amazement. She knew at that moment that she would be with him forever. No matter what. They had to be together. It was impossible.

It made no sense. She knew he wasn't a part of her world and she knew nothing of his life before a few weeks ago. It didn't make sense. Still, it didn't matter. She loved him and she would make it work.

She dropped the roses and rested in his embrace. She liked the smooth masculine feel of his suit as his arms pressed her to him. "Yes," she whispered inaudibly.

He drew her face up to his. His eyes searched hers briefly, then he kissed her long and tenderly. This was the magic electricity she had felt while she danced. As she responded his kiss became fierce and demanding. He broke from her, leaving her gasping.

"I can't ask you to give this up," he said. "That's what I came here for. To chase you down and drag you back to Texas for your own good whether you wanted to go or not. But I see now I can't."

She tried to speak but he hushed her. "No, it doesn't matter. I understand now. When I saw the way you moved on that stage, I understood your need for it."

He laughed. "And I understood ballet for the first time in my life."

She reached for him. "Blackburn, I always wanted—"

He shook his head, stopping her. "No, let me say it all. I'm sorry I didn't trust you the way I asked you to trust me. You don't know what happened to me back when. . . . But I was a jerk. I know you better than that. I'm sorry I wasn't happy for you that day. I should have known you couldn't leave Mantilla Bluff without . . . " He sighed in frustration.

"I'm not leaving Mantilla Bluff," Andrea said, smiling at him.

"No, I know you love me, but I can't ask you to give up what you were born for," he said softly.

"It's not all I was born for." She caressed his muscular arms and chest, revelling in his warm strength.

"No," he repeated, "you're too good at this. And you'd have regrets just like your mother did."

"That was different," she protested. "She hadn't had a chance to do anything yet, but look at all I've been able to achieve."

Her voice changed from urgency to tenderness. "You're right; I am good and I love my work. But I love you more. I've had the best of both worlds and I know what I want.

"I can live without ballet. I can't live without you."

She slid a hand around his neck and stood en pointe to kiss him. He yielded to her gratefully, then his hands clamped firmly around her arms and he set her down on her heels again.

"No, Andrea, no." The words were low and deadly earnest. "You will not do this. I won't let you give this up for me. I love you!" He pushed away from her and turned, searching for an exit.

Andrea grabbed a fistful of lapel and jerked him back to face her. "Yeah? What are you gonna do about it, besides pitch a fit at me?"

He frowned into her eyes for a long moment. She saw tortured longing and pain in his, then understanding and resignation.

"How can I run a Texas ranch—two Texas ranches— if I'm living in Massachusetts?"

She remained persistent. "I don't know. How can you?"

"I've lived in the East and done the whole high-pressure, congested, high-speed bit. I ended up limping home in defeat."

"That was then, this is now." Andrea shoved him away angrily. "That was her. This is me, Blackburn."

Their anger and passion were frozen in time for a moment as they stared at each other. Blackburn ran a hand over his face, smoothing the tension out of his features. He hung his head back and sighed. "I'm going to hate living in Boston. Just don't try to make me eat scrod."

Andrea laughed and threw her arms around him. She was right to love this man, this wonderful, intelligent, complicated, giving man.

"You won't hate living in Boston with me, I promise. A professional dancer is like a professional athlete," she explained. "The career can only last so long before the knees go. I should have another few good performing years. Then I think we should go back to Mantilla Bluff."

"I'll still have to go back to the ranch from time to time," he said. "It'll cost us a fortune but I guess I can be a long-distance commuter. We can spend the summers there, can't we?"

She shook her head. "No, we're going on tour, but it will be a wonderful honeymoon. I'll show you Europe."

"*You* show me? No, *I'll* show you Europe. I know all the quaint, curious little places on the continent you tourists never see."

She began to walk him back to her dressing room. They drank in each other, paying no attention to the bustling activity around them.

"Ah, yes, Blackburn on the continent. But ex-spies have to keep a low profile," she teased. "Where did you serve? Why did you quit?"

"I'll tell you the whole tragic story sometime."

She opened the dressing room door to see it filled with bouquets and gifts. In the center was a small arrangement with prairie grasses and sage woven into the roses. The scent took her back to Mantilla Bluff and a night of bright moonlight and warm breezes. She snapped off a piece of sage and held the pale green twig to her nose. She looked at him over it.

"I was thinking," she said, "with a wooden floor built over the stone, Mantilla Bluff would make a good performance space."

He liked that idea. "You could teach," he said.

"No, teaching takes a special talent that I don't really think I have. Besides, after the babies come I'll want to spend as much time enjoying them as I can."

He was blushing under his deep tan and she laughed. "But I was thinking too that since we have all that space. . . . Of course, we'll have to add some facilities, but that shouldn't be any real problem. We have a perfect location for a summer dance institute. Provide a real, intensive, professional workshop for young performers. Doesn't that sound exciting?"

"It does for a fact. It sounds like a perfect life." He took her in his arms and kissed her again, clinging to her as if she were the very breath of his life.

These kisses possess me completely, she thought.

"There is just one question," she said gravely. "What is your name?"

His laughter shook the tiny room. "Every good Texas family has to have a Travis in it."

"Travis," she repeated. "Travis Blackburn, I love you."